Leona's Unlucky Mission

Shana Muldoon Zappa and Ahmet Zappa

with Zelda Rose

PaRRagon

Bath · New York · Cologne · Melbourne · Delhi
Hong Kong · Shenzhen · Singapore

Leona's Unlucky Mission

This edition published by Parragon Books Ltd in 2016

Parragon Books Ltd
Chartist House
15–17 Trim Street
Bath BA1 1HA, UK
www.parragon.com

ISBN 978-1-4748-4086-6

Printed in UK

To our beautiful, sweet treasure,
Halo Violetta Zappa. You are pure light and joy
and our greatest inspiration. We love you soooo much.

May every step upon your path be blessed with positivity and
the understanding that you have the power within you to
manifest the most fulfilling life you can possibly imagine and
more. May you always remember that being different and true
to your highest self makes your inner star shine brighter.

Remember that you have the power of choice.... Choose thoughts
that feel good. Choose love and friendships that feed your spirit.
Choose actions for peace and nourishment. Choose boundaries
for the same. Choose what speaks to your creativity and unique
inner voice ... what truly makes you happy. And always know
that no matter what you choose, you are unconditionally loved.

Look up to the stars and know you are never alone.
When in doubt, go within ... the answers are all there.
Smiles light the world and laughter is the best medicine.
And NEVER EVER stop making wishes....

Glow for it....
Mummy and Daddy

And to everyone else here on 'Wishworld':

May you realize that no matter where you are in life, no
matter what you look like or where you were born, you, too,
have the power within you to create the life of your dreams.
Through celebrating your own uniqueness, thinking positively,
and taking action, you can make your wishes come true.

Smile. The Star Darlings have your back.
We know how startastic you truly are.

Glow for it....
Your friends,
Shana and Ahmet

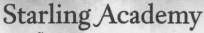

Starling Academy

NAME: Clover
BRIGHT DAY: 5th January
FAVOURITE COLOUR: Purple
INTERESTS: Music, painting and studying
WISH: To be the best songwriter and DJ on Starland
WHY CHOSEN: Clover has great self-discipline, patience and willpower. She is creative, responsible, dependable and extremely loyal.
WATCH OUT FOR: Clover can be hard to read and she is reserved with those she doesn't know. She's afraid to take risks and can be a wisecracker at times.
SCHOOL YEAR: Second
POWER CRYSTAL: Panthera
WISH PENDANT: Hair clip

NAME: Adora
BRIGHT DAY: 14th February
FAVOURITE COLOUR: Sky blue
INTERESTS: Science and thinking about the future and how she can make it better
WISH: To be the top fashion designer on Starland
WHY CHOSEN: Adora is clever and popular and cares about the world around her. She's a deep thinker.
WATCH OUT FOR: Adora can have her head in the clouds and be thinking about other things.
SCHOOL YEAR: Third
POWER CRYSTAL: Azurica
WISH PENDANT: Watch

NAME: Piper
BRIGHT DAY: 4th March
FAVOURITE COLOUR: Sea-foam green
INTERESTS: Composing poetry and writing in her dream journal
WISH: To become the best version of herself she can possibly be and to share that by writing books
WHY CHOSEN: Piper is giving, kind and sensitive. She is very intuitive and aware.
WATCH OUT FOR: Piper can be dreamy, absent-minded and wishy-washy. She can also be moody and easily swayed by the opinions of others.
SCHOOL YEAR: Second
POWER CRYSTAL: Dreamalite
WISH PENDANT: Bracelets

Student Reports

NAME: Astra
BRIGHT DAY: 9th April
FAVOURITE COLOUR: Red
INTERESTS: Individual sports
WISH: To be the best athlete on Starland — to win!
WHY CHOSEN: Astra is energetic, brave, clever and confident. She has boundless energy and is always direct and to the point.
WATCH OUT FOR: Astra is sometimes cocky, self-centred, condescending and brash.
SCHOOL YEAR: Second
POWER CRYSTAL: Quarrelite
WISH PENDANT: Wristbands

NAME: Tessa
BRIGHT DAY: 18th May
FAVOURITE COLOUR: Emerald green
INTERESTS: Food, flowers and love
WISH: To be successful enough so she can enjoy a life of luxury
WHY CHOSEN: Tessa is warm, charming, affectionate, trustworthy and dependable. She has incredible drive and commitment.
WATCH OUT FOR: Tessa does not like to be rushed. She can be quite stubborn and often says no. She does not deal well with change and is prone to exaggeration. She can be easily sidetracked.
SCHOOL YEAR: Third
POWER CRYSTAL: Gossamer
WISH PENDANT: Brooch

NAME: Gemma
BRIGHT DAY: 2nd June
FAVOURITE COLOUR: Orange
INTERESTS: Sharing her thoughts about almost anything
WISH: To be valued for her opinions on everything
WHY CHOSEN: Gemma is friendly, easygoing, funny, extroverted and sociable. She knows a little bit about everything.
WATCH OUT FOR: Gemma talks — a lot — and can be a little too honest sometimes and offend others. She has a short attention span and can be superficial.
SCHOOL YEAR: First
POWER CRYSTAL: Scatterite
WISH PENDANT: Earrings

Starling Academy

NAME: Cassie
BRIGHT DAY: 6th July
FAVOURITE COLOUR: White
INTERESTS: Reading and crafting
WISH: To be more independent and confident, and less fearful
WHY CHOSEN: Cassie is extremely imaginative and artistic. She is a voracious reader and is loyal, caring and a good friend. She is very intuitive.
WATCH OUT FOR: Cassie can be distrustful, jealous, moody and brooding.
SCHOOL YEAR: First
POWER CRYSTAL: Lunalite
WISH PENDANT: Glasses

NAME: Leona
BRIGHT DAY: 16th August
FAVOURITE COLOUR: Gold
INTERESTS: Acting, performing and dressing up
WISH: To be the most famous pop star on Starland
WHY CHOSEN: Leona is confident, hardworking, generous, open-minded, optimistic, caring and a strong leader.
WATCH OUT FOR: Leona can be vain, opinionated, selfish, bossy, dramatic and stubborn, and she is prone to losing her temper.
SCHOOL YEAR: Third
POWER CRYSTAL: Glisten paw
WISH PENDANT: Cuff

NAME: Vega
BRIGHT DAY: 1st September
FAVOURITE COLOUR: Blue
INTERESTS: Exercising, analysing, cleaning and solving puzzles
WISH: To be the top student at Starling Academy
WHY CHOSEN: Vega is reliable, observant, organized and focused.
WATCH OUT FOR: Vega can be opinionated about everything, and she can be fussy, uptight, critical, arrogant and easily embarrassed.
SCHOOL YEAR: Second
POWER CRYSTAL: Queezle
WISH PENDANT: Belt

Student Reports

NAME: Libby
BRIGHT DAY: 12th October
FAVOURITE COLOUR: Pink
INTERESTS: Helping others, interior design, art and dancing
WISH: To give everyone what they need — both on Starland and through wish granting on Wishworld
WHY CHOSEN: Libby is generous, articulate, gracious, diplomatic and kind.
WATCH OUT FOR: Libby can be indecisive and may try too hard to please everyone.
SCHOOL YEAR: First
POWER CRYSTAL: Charmelite
WISH PENDANT: Necklace

NAME: Scarlet
BRIGHT DAY: 3rd November
FAVOURITE COLOUR: Black
INTERESTS: Crystal climbing (and other extreme sports), magic and thrill seeking
WISH: To live on Wishworld
WHY CHOSEN: Scarlet is confident, intense, passionate, magnetic, curious and very brave.
WATCH OUT FOR: Scarlet is a loner and can alienate others by being secretive, arrogant, stubborn and jealous.
SCHOOL YEAR: Third
POWER CRYSTAL: Ravenstone
WISH PENDANT: Boots

NAME: Sage
BRIGHT DAY: 1st December
FAVOURITE COLOUR: Lavender
INTERESTS: Travel, adventure, telling stories, nature and philosophy
WISH: To become the best Wish-Granter Starland has ever seen
WHY CHOSEN: Sage is honest, adventurous, curious, optimistic, friendly and relaxed.
WATCH OUT FOR: Sage has a quick temper! She can also be restless, irresponsible and too trusting of others' opinions. She may jump to conclusions.
SCHOOL YEAR: First
POWER CRYSTAL: Lavenderite
WISH PENDANT: Necklace

Introduction

You take a deep breath, about to blow out the candles on your birthday cake. Clutching a coin in your fist, you get ready to toss it into the dancing waters of a fountain. You stare at your little brother as you each hold the end of a dried wishbone, about to pull. But what do you do first?

You make a wish, of course!

Ever wonder what happens right after you make that wish? *Not much*, you may be thinking.

Well, you'd be wrong.

Because something quite unexpected happens next. Each and every wish that is made becomes a glowing Wish Orb, invisible to the human eye. This undetectable orb zips through the air and into the heavens, on a one-way trip to the brightest star in the sky – a magnificent place called Starland. Starland is inhabited by Starlings, who look a lot like you and me, except they have a sparkly glow to their skin, and glittery hair in unique colours. And they have one more thing: magical powers. The Starlings use these powers to make good wishes come true, for when good wishes are granted, it results in positive energy. And the Starlings of Starland need this energy to keep their world running.

In case you are wondering, there are three kinds of Wish Orbs:

1) GOOD WISH ORBS. These wishes are positive and helpful and come from the heart. They are pretty and sparkly and are nurtured in climate-controlled Wish-Houses. They bloom into fantastical glowing orbs. When the time is right, they are presented to the appropriate Starling for wish fulfilment.

2) BAD WISH ORBS. These are for selfish, mean-spirited or negative things. They don't

sparkle at all. They are immediately transported to a special containment centre, as they are very dangerous and must not be granted.

3) IMPOSSIBLE WISH ORBS. These wishes are for things like world peace, curing diseases and unattainable requests that simply can't be granted by Starlings. These sparkle with an almost impossibly bright light and are taken to a special area of the Wish-House with tinted windows to contain the glare they produce. The hope is that one day they can be turned into good wishes the Starlings can help grant.

Starlings take their wish granting very seriously. There is a special school, called Starling Academy, that accepts only the best and brightest young Starling girls. They study hard for four years, and when they graduate, they are ready to start travelling to Wishworld to help grant wishes. For as long as anyone can remember, only graduates of wish-granting schools have ever been allowed to travel to Wishworld. But things have changed in a very big way.

Read on for the rest of the story....

Prologue

Dear Mum and Dad,

First, star salutations for the parcel! How did you know I needed a new toothlight? (Why are they so easy to lose?) And, Mum, your gamma-chip clusters are out of this world! I've already eaten half the box. They're soooooo starlicious I just can't stop! I know you said to share them with my roommate, Scarlet, and I would have, but guess what? She had to move out. Long story. (Don't worry, it wasn't my fault.) The good news is — you remember how she used to skateboard down the walls? Well, she won't be doing that any more, at least not in my room! So for now I've got the whole room to myself – and it looks soooo much better without all that black! I'm hoping to get a new roommate soon, though, and I'll let you know when I do. Stars crossed she's into a colour that goes a little bit better with gold – and that she's a lot more relaxed and not so hard to talk to.

Oh, and guess what! More big news! I formed a new band!!!!!! It's called Star Darlings! And I'm the lead singer (of course)! We haven't played a gig yet, but I know we will, and I'll send you a holo-vid as soon as we do. We even have a manager, so it's the real deal! Remember Clover? Her colour is purple and she wears the hat? Anyway, her family is the Flying Molensas – as in the circus we used to go to every year! So she knows all about show business and she writes great songs. I know you keep saying that becoming a pop star is a moon shot, and that chances are a hydrong to one, but I have a starmendous feeling about us! And I might as well shoot for the stars, right? Isn't that what they're for?

Speaking of stars, I was looking at Grandpa's the other day, and I swear it winked at me!

Tell Felix congratulations on his promotion to assistant manager of the shoe shop. (I won't mention that Dad is his boss.) And tell Garfield I'll believe *he has a girlfriend when he sends me a holo-pic. I'm waiting! (Ha-ha!)*

Finally, tell Duchess and Francesca I'll holo-call them tonight if I have the chance. There's a first-year student here named Cassie who reminds me so much of Duchess, by the way. She has the same thick black lashes and soft rosy eyes. She's like a little doll you just want to pick up and hug!

I miss you and I love you.

Your superstar,

Leona

P.S. Send more clusters when you can!

Leona read over her holo-letter quickly, trying to think of what else to say. She tried to send one to her parents weekly, though sometimes she forgot. Sometimes, too, it was nearly impossible to write anything without giving her Star Darlings identity away. For instance, how could she explain Scarlet's moving out without mentioning that Scarlet had been dismissed from the group? She sent her letter with a flick of her wrist. Hopefully, one day they'd all be able to share their secret with their families, but who knew when that would be?

CHAPTER

1

Twinkle, twinkle. TWINKLE, TWINKLE. *Twinkle, twinkle.*

That was the sound of a Star-Zap that had been trying to get its owner's attention for quite some time. Leona, who was getting ready for bed in the blissful peace of a roommate-less dorm room, had stopped singing into her hairbrush for a moment to actually run it through her hair, and she finally heard the insistent sound. She grabbed her Star-Zap eagerly, willing it to be news of another Wish Mission, hopefully hers. But her brow wrinkled in confusion as she read the message: PLEASE COME TO MY OFFICE IMMEDIATELY. I HAVE A MATTER OF GREAT URGENCY TO DISCUSS WITH YOU. LADY STELLA. Leona, already dressed in gold-decorated pyjama bottoms and a golden vest top, threw on a dressing gown made of the softest glimmerworm silk, shoved her feet into a pair of golden flats, and raced out of the door, feeling a heady mix of excitement, anticipation and dread. As she hurried along on the Cosmic Transporter, she thought of what it could be. Would Scarlet be reinstated as a Star Darling (and be her roommate once more)? Maybe it would be Libby's Wish Blossom presentation (which had been postponed due to the Scarlet situation). Or what if someone had caught wind of their secret trips to Wishworld? She shook her head, clearing it. No, she decided, it was none of those. Then she had another thought, which made her heart beat double time: maybe she was going to be awarded some honour. Possibly Most Popular Starling Academy Student or Most Likely to Be a Shining Star.

Leona arrived at Lady Stella's office door with a big smile on her face, in case any holo-pictures were to be taken. She chided herself for not changing her outfit into something a little less slumberrific.

The door to Lady Stella's office was ajar. That was odd. Leona walked inside the grand space she had come to know quite well. In the very centre stood the round table where they had first met together as a team. There sat three of her fellow Star Darlings.

They looked at her nervously. "Where is everyone?" Leona asked. Sage, Vega and Libby looked up at her and shrugged silently.

"I was kind of hoping this was going to be my Wish Blossom presentation," Libby said, twirling a strand of her pretty pink hair round her finger. "But then where's everyone else?" She looked around the office as if the other girls were hiding behind the furniture and would soon pop out to surprise her.

Lady Stella strode into the room, followed by Lady Cordial, the head of admissions. Lady Cordial was one of a handful of Starling Academy administrators who knew of the Star Darlings' and Lady Stella's plan. Smiling tightly, as she always did, she greeted the Star Darlings with clasped hands and a tidy bow. Lady Stella used her wish energy to close the door behind them – a little more forcefully than necessary, in Leona's opinion.

Leona couldn't help admiring Lady Stella, who was so lithe and beautiful. The headmistress was as regal and confident as the head of admissions was meek and nervous. Then Leona took a closer look at Lady Stella. In her two plus years at Starling Academy, Leona had never seen the woman look so ... so ... irritated. It couldn't be good news. Lady Stella looked at the four girls. "Where's Scarlet?" she asked.

Leona shrugged. "I haven't seen her since she moved out of our room," she said. The other girls nodded in agreement.

"Really?" said Lady Stella. Her smooth forehead creased with concern. "That is surprising. We had a lengthy discussion after everything happened and she was very gracious. I'm surprised she didn't respond to my holo-text."

Scarlet? Gracious? thought Leona. She'd have to take the headmistress's word for it.

Libby shook her head. "It's true. We haven't seen her anywhere," she said. "Not at lunch or at band practice."

Sage spoke up. "She missed our Wish Probability class, and study group, too."

Lady Stella frowned. "I see ... I suppose it's entirely possible that Scarlet was more upset than she let on." She inhaled sharply. "Perhaps it's no surprise that a Starling would need some time alone."

Especially Scarlet, thought Leona. *She never seemed particularly eager to be around the other Starlings before anyway.*

She stood, thinking the meeting was over.

"Not so fast, Leona," said Lady Stella. "I haven't got to the reason I summoned you all here."

Leona sat down with a thump.

"I have two words for you girls," the headmistress said grimly. "Star Darlings."

The girls looked at her blankly. She continued. "What in the stars were you thinking, naming your band after our secret group?"

Leona gasped. She had been so excited about being named the lead singer of the band that the actual name had barely registered with her at the time. It *was* strange, come to think of it. Quickly she explained to Lady Stella exactly what had happened, and the other girls broke in and added their own thoughts. Leona had always wanted to start a rock band – since her younger years, in fact, back in Flairfield – so that she could be the lead singer, of course. And as soon as Lady Stella formed the Star Darlings, Leona couldn't help thinking that it would be the perfect place to start.

Many of the Star Darlings already played instruments, Leona knew, and it would be a startastic way to get to know each other even better than they already did.

There were never supposed to be open auditions. That was something Leona had thought she'd made perfectly clear. Somehow, though – it was still a mystery – a holo-flyer had been sent out to every Star-Zap in the school. Except the Star Darlings' Star-Zaps, which just made everything even weirder. Worse was that Leona couldn't even pick the band members in the end, even though it had all been her idea. Starling Academy rules – ever fair and balanced and just – stipulated that any audition on school property be overseen by a school official using a Ranker, a judging machine designed to be completely objective and keep any contest a hydrong per cent fair.

So the Ranker had chosen a group of girls and also the name of the band. And it just so happened that the five girls who were chosen were all Star Darlings, and that the name it picked was ... the Star Darlings.

Lady Stella shook her head. "This is very odd indeed."

Lady Cordial piped up, "S-s-s-s-so very s-s-s-s-strange Lady Stella. S-s-s-s-so very s-s-s-s-strange."

Lady Stella looked at the girls and her expression softened. "So you girls had nothing to do with this?" They shook their heads.

"And who was the professor in charge?" Lady Stella asked.

Leona thought. "It was Professor ... Professor Leticia Langtree."

Lady Cordial touched Lady Stella's arm, and the headmistress bent down so the shorter woman could whisper in her ear. Lady Stella listened, nodded, then straightened, her mouth set in a grim line. "I will make a delicate inquiry with her to determine if this was a random mistake or done deliberately." She shook her head. "But really, what are the chances of a Ranker picking the same secret name?" she mused aloud. "What are the chances?"

Her question was rhetorical, but Starlings are born with an innate knowledge of mathematics, and the answer was on the tips of their tongues in no time. "One in five hydrong mooniums," everyone chorused.

As they stood and began filing out of the room, Lady Stella was shaking her head. "The revelation of your group's secret name is very concerning to me. Very concerning."

Leona and the rest of the band walked down the hallway, nobody saying a word. They stepped out into the still night, the sky clear and filled with twinkling stars. They all paused for a moment, looking up and taking it all in. Most of their other classmates were already in bed, dreaming their Starling dreams as they absorbed their lessons for the day. Then, without a word, the four Star Darlings headed to the campus Cosmic Transporter, the moving pavement that whisked Starlings across the school grounds. It wasn't until they were moving towards the dorms that Leona broke the silence.

"So what?" she said. "What is the big deal that our name is out there? I mean, we're still secretly going on missions. That hasn't changed. I think Lady Stella is totally overreacting," she said firmly.

Vega shook her blue-bobbed head from side to side. "I don't know, Leona. Lady Stella seemed pretty upset. There must be more to it."

"Time will tell," said Sage wearily. "Time will tell."

And with that, the four girls went their separate ways to try to get some sleep.

CHAPTER
2

BAM!

Leona looked up. What had that been? Had it come from the hall? It was always so quiet. Intrigued, Leona jumped off the bed to see what was going on.

Leona ran to her door and pulled it open – just a crack. She peered down the hall to see Tessa, fists clenched, facing her own door. Tessa seemed about to tell the door something, but she changed her mind and turned away. Leona watched for another starmin as Tessa stomped on to the dorm's Cosmic Transporter. Bright green sparkles flew from her hair as it swung back and forth.

Tessa could be stubborn, Leona knew, but this was a side she'd never seen before. In fact, in the two-plus staryears they'd been together at Starling Academy,

Leona had never witnessed Tessa losing her cool, not once. Not even with Gemma, her younger sister – a first-year student and their fellow Star Darling – whose mouth was as big as Wishworld's sun. No, Tessa was always the even-tempered Starling, the peacemaker if anyone quarrelled. Her roommate, Adora, must have done something pretty outrageous to get a reaction like *that* out of her.

Twinkle, twinkle.

On her desk, Leona's Star-Zap rang. A holo-call was coming in. She dashed back to answer it. "Star greetings?"

Her fellow Star Darling Cassie popped up, waving. "It's me," Cassie chirped. She was in her reading nook in her dorm room, surrounded by star-shaped quilted pillows and piles of holo-books and holo-magazines. "So, have you heard anything more from Scarlet? I'm worried about her, aren't you?"

"I guess." Leona shrugged. "Right now, though, I'm much more interested in this fight Adora and Tessa just had."

"Fight? Tessa and Adora?" Cassie's pale skin shimmered in her surprise.

Leona made an X on her chest. "Cross my stars and hope to shine."

"Moon and stars…. What happened?"

"I don't know. All I saw was Tessa storming down the hall."

Just then, a tiny star flashed in the upper corner of her Star-Zap, indicating that lunch would soon be served.

"Lunchtime already?" exclaimed Leona. "Sunspots! Where did the morning go? I still have to take a sparkle shower! Give me 10 starmins, and I'll meet you outside, between the dorms."

Freshly sparkling and dressed in her favourite gold tunic, marigold-coloured leggings and golden boots, Leona joined Cassie in the courtyard between their neighbouring dorms. Cassie, who was just in her first year at Starling Academy, shared a room with Sage, their fellow Star Darling, in the Little Dipper Dorm. The building was where all first- and second-year students lived. As a third year, Leona lived with all third- and fourth-year Starlings in the only slightly larger but more luxurious Big Dipper Dorm.

Arm in arm, as was the custom for Starlings whenever travelling in pairs, they strode past the Star Quad, the star-shaped heart of the Starling Academy campus, where the iconic dancing fountain cheerfully sparkled and splashed. Just past the quad rose the semi-star-shaped band shell, Leona's favourite place on campus apart from her room. Her brand-new band hadn't played there yet, but they would soon. A few more practices and they'd be ready to take the stage and rock the school!

Behind the band shell stood the academy's enormous dining hall, the Celestial Café. In case anyone missed the signal on her Star-Zap, a great glowing star above the door flashed, announcing mealtime to everyone.

Inside the vast, warmly lit dining room, which was somehow cosy and elegant all at once, Leona and Cassie joined Piper and Gemma, their fellow Star Darlings who were already seated at the table the group had made their own. Ever since they'd been chosen, the girls had eaten their meals together at the table by the window with what many thought was one of the best views from the school. Gazing out, one could see both the jewel-like Crystal Mountains and the glistening, violet-hued Luminous Lake. These beautiful landmarks were the pride and joy of Starland City. Still, Leona personally enjoyed the view from her own dorm room window even more: it was of the glimmering skyline of downtown Starland City, the place she'd grown up dreaming about moving to – as a superstar, of course!

Before the girls could even exchange star greetings, a Bot-Bot waiter appeared. It filled their crystal goblets with sparkling water and placed a piping-hot roll fresh from the oven for each of them on their china plates.

"Star greetings, Leona, Cassie. What is it that you desire?" asked the Bot-Bot waiter.

"Hmm ... let's see...." Leona's forehead wrinkled. What would she have that day?

There was no menu for them to choose from. They could order anything their hearts desired, and Leona prided herself on never having ordered something more than once since she had been at Starling Academy.

"A garble-green soufflé for me, please," said Cassie.

"Really? Again? You don't get tired of that?" Leona asked.

"Not really," said Cassie. "It's tasty. And it's healthy. Why mess with something that works?"

Leona cocked her head and grinned, waggling her eyebrows. "I don't know ... because you *can*?"

"And for you, Leona?" The Bot-Bot waiter hovered politely near her shoulder, ready to transmit her request to the café's gourmet Bot-Bot chefs.

"Right ... okay ... for me.... What are you having?" Leona asked Piper, eyeing the glossy emerald tendrils piled on her plate.

"Who, me? Oh, a starweed salad."

Leona scrunched up her nose. "Hmm ... I'll pass. What about you?" She turned to Gemma.

"Me? A druderwomp burger," said Gemma, moving in for another bite.

"Ah! Now that's a vegetable I like! I think I'll have that, a druderwomp burger – well done – with extra mooncheese. I haven't had that before, have I?"

The Bot-Bot waiter scanned its memory to check. "No," it replied decidedly. "Never with extra cheese."

"Starmendous. Star salutations." Leona thanked their server with a wave. "*Soooo?*" she went on, gazing around. "Where's everyone else?"

"Well, we know where Scarlet's *not*," said Gemma as a glob of bright orange mustardia-blossom sauce dribbled down her chin and on to her shirt. She glanced down, not sure where to wipe, since it was the same colour as her top.

"Well, *that* I knew," said Leona. "You do know she's moved out of my room?"

"Really?" said Gemma. "Already?"

Leona nodded. "Completely. Everything's gone. Not a speck of hot pink or black. It's like she was never there." She smiled.

"Ah, but she was. Don't forget that," said Piper.

"Uh, I wasn't going to. But star salutations."

Piper tossed her pale green hair over her shoulder. "You're welcome," she replied.

Cassie spoke up. "Well, Scarlet still has to eat. Even if she's not a Star Darling, she's still a student. Is she sitting with someone else?"

The dining room was so vast it was hard to identify each and every sparkling face. But Scarlet had always stood out in a crowd in her palette of hot pink and jet black. The four Star Darlings scanned the wavy rows of tables. One by one, each shook her head. If Scarlet had been in the café, they would have spotted her in the rainbow of students, without a doubt.

"It wouldn't be the first meal she ever skipped," said Leona. "You know how antisocial she can be. Honestly, I never could see how Lady Stella ever sensed Star Darling potential in her, let alone see her granting wishes."

"Well, don't tell Libby that," Gemma warned. "She's really upset about the whole thing. And her stars get out of line so easily lately. You'd think a successful mission would have helped, but *nooooo*," Gemma groaned. "Honestly, I don't know how much longer I can share a room with her."

"Hey, here come Clover and Astra," observed Piper, pointing with her chin.

Leona and the others turned, eager to find out what news the second-year roommates might have. If they did have any, though, it didn't look like it was very good.

"What's wrong?" Cassie asked as they reached the table.

Clover shrugged and nodded towards Astra. "Ask her."

"No, ask her." Astra slid her warm auburn eyes to Clover. "Seriously, what were we fighting about again?"

"Well ... if I remember correctly, you were cheating."

"But I wasn't."

"But you were."

"Oh, just admit it, Astra," Gemma cut in. "Everyone knows you hate to lose."

Astra glared down her nose at the ginger-haired Starling. Her own flame-red hair flickered indignantly. "That doesn't mean I'd cheat, Gemma. Who asked you, anyway?"

"Could somebody please start from the beginning?" said Cassie.

"It's no big deal," said Clover, shrugging the whole episode away. She shook off her plum jacket and tossed it over the back of her chair. With a flick of her head, she shook her violet fringe out of her eyes and sank into her seat. "I'm not even mad ... any more.... We were playing a friendly game of holo-cards in our room, and Astra cheated. The end."

"But I didn't cheat," groaned Astra. "I mean, what kind of Starling do you think I am? Besides, Clover, I didn't even need to cheat to win. You tried to shoot the moon when you knew I'd broken hearts."

"Let's just forget about it," said Clover, bowing her head.

"You know, I was kind of missing having a roommate," said Leona, chuckling. "But not so much any more."

"It's not funny," Piper said, leaning intently over her salad. "I don't know if you Starlings have noticed it, but lately I've been sensing a lot of tension in the air, including from my own roommate, Vega. She wasn't talking to me this morning when she left. In fact –" Piper frowned and slowly sat back, "I wonder if that's why she's not here, because she's still so mad...."

"Like Tessa and Adora!" exclaimed Cassie.

"What about Tessa?" Gemma's ears glistened at her sister's name.

By that time, though, a duo of Bot-Bot waiters had returned to take Clover and Astra's orders and serve Leona and Cassie's food.

"Mmm! Star salutations!" Leona licked her lips and used her wish energy manipulation skills to mentally flick open her napkin, a crisp cloth square, which she then laid across her lap. "Could we worry about all that stuff later and worry about eating right now?" she begged.

CHAPTER
3

In the end, there was no discussion of Star Darlings tension, because the rest of the girls soon arrived and the talk at the lunch table shifted quickly to Scarlet and her dismissal and, most importantly, what it meant. Did it really matter that there were only 11 of them now?

"I don't see why it would," Leona said. "We'll just all go on more missions. We can pick up one Starling's slack. Especially a Starling like Scarlet. I never trusted her anyway."

"Oh, Leona!" Libby's eyes flashed protectively across the table. "That's a terrible thing to say."

"Star apologies," muttered Leona. "But you didn't live with her.... I'm just saying I wasn't surprised."

Sage, meanwhile, tugged on her lavender plaits, thinking. "Remember what Lady Stella told us all when she met with us for the first time? If we didn't want to be part of this mission, she would find another Starling who did. What if she's finding another one right now to make us 12 again?"

"Maybe...." Vega nodded.

"Well, I'm going to miss her," Libby said, "even if she did say more with her drums than she ever did with her mouth. I mean, she used to –"

"Wait! Hold your stars! What did you say?" Leona gasped. How in the universe had she gone so long without considering what losing Scarlet really and truly might mean?

"What are you talking about?" asked Libby.

"Drums!" Leona gulped. "Maybe our mission can succeed without Scarlet. But what about my band?"

Leona had hoped against hope that Scarlet would show up for their usual band practice, but she didn't, to no one's surprise. The rest of them – Sage on guitar, Vega on bass, Libby on keytar and Leona on vocals – waited for a few starmins in their Lightning Lounge rehearsal room, tuning up and trading riffs.

Suddenly, a scowling face framed by a blue fringe appeared in the doorway, which Leona had left open –

for Scarlet, she had hoped. She regretted the mistake immediately and reached out the hand that wasn't holding her microphone to wave the rehearsal-room door closed.

Unfortunately, because Vivica, the nosy Starling, was standing in its way, the door politely refused to close on her, which was how doors on Starland worked.

"We're busy," Leona growled.

Her bandmates nodded.

Vivica was just about the only Starling at Starling Academy who no one liked having around.

"Busy doing what? Not making music, that's for sure," Vivica said, laughing. She closed her eyes, enjoying her joke.

"What we need is a little privacy," snapped Leona.

"We're rehearsing," Libby explained. She even flashed Vivica a generous star-salutations-for-understanding-now-please-get-out-of-here grin.

Instead of backing out of the doorway, though, Vivica glided in.

"Oh ... is this your little band?" She fired a look at each of them: Libby, Vega, Sage and Leona. "I thought you had a drummer, too."

"She's late." "She quit." "She's missing." "We do."

The whole band answered Vivica at the same time with four different replies.

"Huh?"

"We don't need a drummer, if that's what you're wondering," said Leona.

Quickly, her bandmates agreed.

"We're good."

"All good."

"Thanks, though," said Libby, who could never stop trying to please.

"I know how badly you wanted to be in the band," Leona said, trying to sound sympathetic as she tossed her mic from hand to hand. "Sorry you didn't make it." She shrugged. "But there's always starchoir, I guess."

Vivica had tried out for the band, along with the hydrongs of other Starlings who had turned up.

Leona could still remember the knots that had formed in her stomach when Vivica stepped on to the band shell to audition – for lead vocals, Leona's own part, no less! Fortunately, the Ranker knew what it was doing and Leona made the band. She'd had to wait stardays for the results, though – the longest stardays of her life.

She could only imagine how disappointed Vivica had been. *She seems to be taking it pretty well now, though*, Leona thought, studying her.

"So, um, this practising you're doing ... when will it be over?" Vivica asked. "I'm wondering because my band needs the practice room today, too."

"Your what?" Leona gasped.

"My band. What?" Vivica's sky-blue lashes fluttered innocently. The ice-blue eyes behind them were less naive. "You think you're the only Starling who can start one? I asked Professor Langtree if the Ranker could rank a second band from the auditions, and she said, 'Sure, why not?'" Vivica's thin blue-lipped smile spread like a stain across her face until it almost reached her ears. "I decided to call it Vivica and the Visionaries. I'm the lead singer, of course, so it makes sense."

Leona didn't turn to see the rest of the band's reaction to this. Her own shock and rage were too strong. "Vivica? And the Visionaries?"

"It's a little more catchy than Star Darlings, don't you think?"

No. What Leona thought was that it was startlingly similar to the name she'd planned to give her own band before the Ranker had named them: Leona and the Luminaries. She'd even started a fan page for them on StarBook before she knew it wouldn't be used. She still hoped the band could change names at some point, but how could they now, when Vivica's band's name was almost the same?

She probably saw the page! Leona thought suddenly. *She probably picked that name out of blue-hearted spite!*

"*Anyway,*" said Vivica, still smiling. "You know, right, that you can only have the rehearsal room for a starhour, max?"

Leona didn't.

"I knew that," Vega said.

"And since it sounds like you can use all the practice time you can get, I guess we'll just come back in a starhour, then."

And with that, Vivica turned, her long pale blue hair swinging behind her back. Leona closed the door with a swipe of her arm, leaving sparks where her hand sliced the air.

"*Starf!*" said Vega. "Two bands. After all these years with none."

"*Grrr!* Can we just play some music," Leona roared, grabbing the mic, "and not talk about other bands?"

Vega gave her bass a half-hearted twirl and started to pluck it, then looked around. "Who's going to count us in?" she asked.

"Oh, for heaven's sake," Leona huffed, "I will. We'll do 'Heart of a Glion' – on three. A-one, a-two ..." She clapped, once, then twice....

On 'three', they began.

"Stop!" Leona yelled, half a verse in. "I can't sing to this. You're all over the place!"

"We need a backbeat," Sage said, sighing.

"Maybe we should call Clover," Vega said.

"Why?" Leona snapped. "So she can write us a new song that doesn't need a beat?"

Clover had been writing songs for staryears and had immediately offered to share them with Leona's brand-new band. She'd even volunteered to be their manager. She was happy to do anything really, except join them on the stage. Even though she had grown up in a huge family of famous circus performers and was very comfortable onstage, she now wished to stay as far from the starlight as possible.

"We need a drummer! Now!" Leona roared. "Or wait ... where's my Star-Zap? Maybe it can play a beat for us? It doesn't quite have the same 'stage presence', but at least it won't sit there sulking like Scarlet," she muttered. "Or get all galactical at the littlest critique...."

"Clover plays the drums," said Vega.

Sage knitted her lilac eyebrows, confused. "I thought she played the guitar."

"Correct," said Vega, "and the drums, and the keyboard and the gammahorn.... You name it." She paused to pluck her instrument. "Including, I'm sure, the bass."

"Are you serious?" Leona said. "Why didn't you say so?"

Had Clover really been letting them play her songs and never once showed off all the musical talent she herself had? *Huh*.... There were so many things about so many Starlings that Leona would never understand.

"Gotcha!" At last, Leona's hand found her Star-Zap in the bottom of her bag. "Clover!" she yelled before the device was even out. "I – make that we – need you in the Lightning Lounge. Now!"

"I'll sit in *today*," said Clover stiffly when she arrived. "But that's it. I'm not performing in public. Ever. Do you understand? When you guys have an actual gig, you'll have to get someone else to play with you. Just so we're perfectly clear." She perched on the stool behind Scarlet's hot-pink drum kit, drumsticks in her hands. She played a tight lick to punctuate her point, then reached up to catch her hat before it tumbled off her head.

"Hey! That was good!" Leona said.

Clover lowered her chin warningly. "Just today," she said, pointing a stick.

"Got it. And star salutations," said Leona, who couldn't have meant it more.

With Clover there, the band's practice went much better. She didn't hit as hard as Scarlet, by any means, but her timing was spot on. Of course, they were playing songs she'd written, so that helped quite a bit.

"Zow! That was stellar!" Sage gushed as their song "White Dwarf" ended. She strummed a joyful extra chord.

"That did sound pretty good," agreed Clover, giving each drumstick a fancy twirl.

Even Libby had to nod appreciatively, though Scarlet's absence still stung her the most.

"I wish we had an audience to hear us!" said Leona.

"Oh, no, you don't," Clover said. "Because then I wouldn't be here. I'm serious. Practice only." *Bam!* She slapped her snare to emphasize her point.

Just then, Sage's pocket began to glow. She let go of her guitar, and while it hovered, twinkling, in front of her body, she pulled out her Star-Zap. Leona stared enviously. Sage was seriously good at wish energy manipulation. And she was only a first year.

"It's a holo-text," she said, "from Cassie."

"What's up?" Leona asked.

Sage's violet eyes grew wider as she read it.

"*What?*" said Leona, straight into the microphone this time.

Cringing, but smiling, too, Sage raised her head. "So, apparently, Cassie was walking by Lady Stella's office, on the way to get her request for a transfer to Advanced Wishworld Lighterature signed by the headmistress. Long story, but apparently, her transcript from her old school somehow, somewhere, got misplaced. Anyway –"

"Yes, *anyway*," said Leona, "get on with this story!"

"Okay, so Cassie says she saw Lady Cordial going into Lady Stella's office ..."

"*Yes?*"

"With a *Starling*! A new *Star Darling*, she thinks!"

"Really? Just now?"

"Mm-hmm."

The bandmates looked at each other.

"Well, what are we waiting for?" Leona said.

CHAPTER
4

Outside the headmistress's office the five musicians found Cassie, propped like a silver statue against the rainbow-grained star-marble wall.

"That was fast!" said Cassie, springing towards them.

"We didn't want to miss anything," Leona said. "So? Are they still in there?"

Cassie nodded. Then, all of a sudden, something caught Cassie's eye. She craned her neck to peer round Leona's back. "What was that?"

"What?" Leona spun round.

"Did the others come with you?"

"No." The bandmates shook their heads.

"Did you text them as well?" asked Sage.

Cassie adjusted her star-shaped glasses. "No ... I only texted you. But I thought I saw someone...." She shrugged. "I'm just nervous, I guess."

"Well, I'm excited!" said Leona. "I wonder who it is. And if she'll be my new roommate, too. Do you have any idea of who it might be?"

"No." Cassie shook her head. "Lady Cordial was in the way, so I couldn't see anything."

Leona thought about who she wouldn't want it to be. "You don't think it's Vivica?" she said as the image of the lead singer of Star Academy's *other* Starling band came to her mind.

There weren't many Starlings at the school who Leona actively tried to avoid. Truth be told, Vivica and now Scarlet were the only ones. Was it because Leona was so competitive? She was, without a doubt. Was it because she and Vivica were rivals, no matter how much the school discouraged that? No. Leona had thought about it. A lot, in fact. She, like so many Starlings, avoided Vivica for one good reason: because Vivica was no fun to be around.

"Oh, starf, I hope not," said Libby.

Just then, a soft *swoosh* made them all turn their heads towards the headmistress's door. As if blown by the wind, it slid open, and Lady Stella's tall, regal form appeared. She wore a silver trouser suit that coordinated beautifully with her perfectly coiffed platinum hair. She smiled at them, and Leona was relieved to see that she didn't seem upset any more. "Why, Sage, Libby, Vega, Leona, Cassie, Clover ..." Her mouth curved up ever so slightly at the corners. "How surprising to find you here."

"Oh ... we're just passing through!" said Leona casually. At least, she hoped it came off that way.

Next to her, Sage nodded. "Just hanging around!" she agreed. "We had no idea you'd be in your office on a starweekend. Is there any ... special reason ... if it's okay to ask?"

Lady Stella's smile warmly spread. Her eyes crinkled at the edges. "As a matter of fact, there is a special reason. A very special one."

Leona and the others waited for her to go on, but instead Lady Stella turned away. They followed her gaze down the hall, where, to their surprise, they saw all five other Star Darlings riding the Cosmic Transporter towards them anxiously.

"You called us, Lady Stella?" panted Tessa. She held up her Star-Zap and pointed to the summons on the screen.

"I did indeed." The headmistress nodded. "I have important news to share."

"Wait ... did our Star-Zaps go off, too?" Leona pulled hers out to check. The screen was blank except for the waning moon in the corner reminding her how much startime until her Advanced Wish Theory project was due.

Sage and the others checked theirs, too. They all looked up, confused.

"I didn't see a need to call you," explained Lady Stella, "since you were already ... 'passing through'. "

With that and a wink, she ushered the Star Darlings into her grand office. Sitting at the table was a small wide-eyed Starling with a galaxy of star-shaped freckles and springy yellow pigtails. Behind her was Lady Cordial, who stood behind the new Starling, her hands grasping the top of the chair the girl sat in.

Leona did not recognize the girl, so she assumed, correctly, that she was a first year. The girl looked like a Starling who was easy to forget – quiet and timid.

"Star Darlings, please, do take your seats," Lady Stella said. She strode to the head of the table and motioned for all of them to sit. Once they had, and the chairs had adjusted to each Starling's height and weight, the headmistress held her hand out gracefully towards the small Starling, sprinkling sparkles from her fingers as she did. "It is my great pleasure to introduce Ophelia, your *true* 12th Star Darling, to the group."

A flurry of gasps and glances swept round the table. Leona's mouth fell ajar.

"*Her?*" blurted Gemma.

"*Shhh!*" Tessa hissed, and rolled her eyes.

"Lady Cordial," said the headmistress, "perhaps you could explain to them."

"Why, yes ... of course. Ahem." The Star Darlings felt for the administrator, whose glow dimmed a humble watt. "It, er, seems, er, that there was a glitch, er, s-s-s-somewhere in our identification program." Lady Cordial paused to swallow her stutter, then dutifully went on. "And as you all know, there was, er, a mix-up in the student list. The *good* news –" she forced a smile; or at least it looked like a smile that was forced, "is that I corrected all the data and was able to get the *right* name."

Lady Cordial moved her hands from the back of Ophelia's chair to Ophelia's shoulders, causing the Starling to jump in her seat. "Ahem. Allow me to introduce your new and true Star Darling, Ophelia. Ophelia ... your Star Darlings team."

Tessa led a round of welcomes while their brand-new member looked from one girl to the next.

"Star greetings," she mumbled back so softly that Leona had to guess that was what she had said.

Lady Stella turned her gaze on her. "Lady Cordial has been making arrangements for Ophelia to be your new roommate, in Scarlet's place."

"Really." Leona's eyes shifted to Ophelia, who raised her hand in a timid wave. "Great." She wasn't exactly the roommate Leona had hoped for, but at least she looked sweet and quiet, which was more than she could say for Scarlet. Actually, she looked like she would be the anti-Scarlet.

"Still no sign of Scarlet?" Lady Stella asked. The Star Darlings shook their heads.

"Well, in any event, our Wish-Watcher is watching a Star Darling Wish Orb at this very moment, which she feels quite sure will be ready to grant soon ... and," she added, "speaking of Wish Orbs, that brings me to the *second* reason I called you all here to my office." She let her eyes orbit the table until they met Libby's rosy ones.

Leona watched Libby's cheeks flush excitedly.

"Well, it's about time!" Libby's roommate, Gemma, declared.

"Gemma! Honestly!" Gemma's sister, Tessa, groaned. "Can you just keep that big orange mouth of yours closed and say nothing for once?"

"No, she's right," Lady Stella said with a gentle nod towards both Gemma and Tessa. "This moment is long overdue." She turned to the others. "In all the ... *confusion* of the other day, I'm afraid, something very important – for Libby especially – was left undone."

"My Wish Blossom," said Libby softly, almost as if it was a secret.

"Indeed." Lady Stella bowed deeply, then gracefully straightened, turned to her desk, and, with a tilt of her head, slid open a drawer. Leona could see the light of the Wish Orb pour out of the drawer the moment it opened, before the orb even came into view.

Carefully, Lady Stella lifted the sparkling orb with both hands and let it rest in her cupped palms like an egg inside a nest. The orb gave out so much light that a shadow appeared on the wall behind her. Its glow lit the headmistress's face like a spotlight, especially her regal cheekbones and her long, slightly upturned nose.

"Rise, Libby, and approach," Lady Stella said slowly, her voice as smooth as polished starjade stone.

Leona watched with a pang of awe and envy as Libby eagerly obeyed. She couldn't help noticing the newest Star Darling, Ophelia, also sitting there gaping at the scene. Her mouth had fallen open and was growing steadily wider.

As soon as Libby reached Lady Stella, the headmistress held out her hands and solemnly waited for Libby to do the same.

"You earned this," said Lady Stella as she placed the glowing orb in Libby's trembling hands. "My deepest star apologies that we had to make you wait."

"Oh! It's heavy!" gasped Libby, clearly surprised, cradling the orb against her chest. "Star salutations," she went on, smiling proudly at the orb. "My aunt always says that anything worth having is worth waiting for.... Oh! I think it's starting to change!"

As Libby spoke, Leona saw the orb's glow getting brighter ... so bright that instead of lighting up the faces of just Lady Stella and Libby, it lit every Star Darling face in the room. Then it happened, just as it had for Sage after her Wish Mission mere stardays before: the orb transformed before all of their eyes from a ball of light into a flower – a delicate scallop-edged, bell-shaped blossom, the same pale pink as a cloud at the end of a Starland sunset, just before lightfall, when the planet seems to awaken and begins to brighten and give off light of its own.

"It's a blushbelle! My favourite!" cooed Libby, leaning in for a deep, blissful sniff. As she did, stardust drifted out from the flower's feathery centre, adding extra sparkle to Libby's face. "Ooh! That tickles!" She rubbed her nose and brushed the loose stardust off her cheeks and chin. "It's so beautiful, isn't it?" Libby went on.

"Indeed, very beautiful ..." Lady Stella agreed, staring at the flower in Libby's hands. Normally, that would have been the end of the wish-granting process; Libby would have had a Wish Blossom to call her own for evermore. But Leona could tell from the way the headmistress seemed to be holding her breath as she gazed into the centre of the blushbelle that she was looking for something else....

"Look inside!" Sage called out. "Do you see anything, Libby? Does it have a stone, like mine did?"

Libby peered into the long cup formed by the petals. "I don't think so...." She shook her head. "I just see more stardust." Then, as if to answer, the pearly pink petals opened wider, trembling teasingly as they did. "Wait. What's happening?"

The petals burst wide open and fell back completely, and where there'd been only stardust, a gleaming stone appeared. It was an angular, glittering, electric-pink jewel that pulsed with an intense inner light. Libby held it in her hand, a quizzical look on her face. "It looks rugged, but it's as light as air," she said in wonder.

"Another stone!" exclaimed Adora.

"It's just like mine!" said Sage. "How do you feel?" she anxiously asked.

Libby thought for a moment. "I feel ... perfectly wonderful!" She closed her eyes and sighed.

"So ... what's with the stones?" asked Leona finally.

Round the table, the other Star Darlings nodded and murmured similar questions. Every face, including Libby's, turned to Lady Stella as they waited to hear.

"That I cannot tell you ... *yet*," she added as 11 faces fell. (Ophelia's, the 12th, was still stuck in its gaping, bewildered stare.) "All in due time," Lady Stella went on with a kind smile and a sweep of her hands.

"But that's what you said the last time," said Leona.

A few Star Darlings turned to her, surprised.

"What?" Leona said. "I mean, that was then and this is now, right? I'm just wondering how long 'due time' takes."

With an almost sad smile, Leona thought, Lady Stella reached for the star-bright stone and plucked it effortlessly from the Wish Blossom's heart. "Due time," she said slowly, "in due time, I fear, Leona. And it is in due time that you will know. Until then ..." She held out the stone for Libby to take, and she took the Wish Blossom from Libby in exchange. "Libby, you performed your mission admirably. You mistook the wish at first, but not in the end. Your mission now is to guard this precious stone with your life. And, of course, continue keeping this secret you've been keeping so well. Now, everyone, watch." The Star Darlings stared as the blushbelle transformed into a Silver Blossom. Lady Stella nodded. "I will save this in our own private Hall of Granted Wishes."

As Libby took the stone and clutched it to her chest, looking rather overcome and overwhelmed, the headmistress turned her full attention to the others. "As I was saying before, a wish has been spotted, correct, Lady Cordial? And it will be ready to grant soon, we think?"

Her tiny colleague replied with an unusually natural smile and a friendly dip of her head. "Yes, Lady Stella. *Very* soon. You are absolutely right."

"So please, Star Darlings, be on high alert for a holo-text summoning you to return. Sage's and Libby's successful missions brought us a lot of positive energy. But there's more work to be done." Lady Stella paused to look round the table and meet each Starling's eyes. Hers were like kaleidoscopes, full of colours, and as soon as they locked on Leona's, Leona felt a surge of confidence and trust.

Ophelia must have felt one even stronger, thought Leona, because after her turn, her eyes shut.

Lady Stella bowed. "Star salutations, Star Darlings."

"Star salutations, Lady Stella."

The Star Darlings rose to go.

"So." Leona waited for Ophelia to circle the table. Now that she was standing next to her, Leona was reminded of how slight Ophelia was. Leona had to bend her neck to meet her eyes. "I guess we're roommates, huh?"

Ophelia nodded.

"Well, come on. Let me show you your new room. What room were you in before? Two fifty-nine? That's on Cassie's floor. How come I've never seen you before?"

Ophelia sighed and shrugged, her yellow pigtails bobbing. "Maybe it's because I'm quiet. No one seems to notice me."

Leona put her arm acround Ophelia . There was something about this little flutterfocus of a Starling that brought out the glioness in her. "I'm sorry, but there is no excuse for not being noticed. Things are going to change."

Ophelia looked up with her wide eyes. "Because I'm a Star Darling now?"

"No," said Leona, tossing her mane. "Because you're my roommate now."

"So ... is it okay if I ask you something?" said Ophelia in a tone that still sounded as if she expected Leona to say no.

"Of course!" said Leona. She squeezed Ophelia's shoulder. "Ask whatever you like."

"Okay...." Ophelia took a deep breath. Her eyes slid to Leona, then darted away. "So ... what exactly happened back there just now?"

Leona squinted. "What happened? I don't get it. Star apologies. What do you mean?"

"I mean ... did that first year, and that other one, did they really grant wishes?" Ophelia asked.

Leona shrugged. "Well, yeah. After all, that's what we do now. That's what this whole Star Darlings thing is. They told you about it all, right? We, *young* Starlings, grant *young* Wishers' wishes and get, like, a hydrong times the positive wish energy. That's Lady Stella's theory, at least."

Ophelia nodded meekly. "Yes. They told me. I guess ... I guess I still don't understand how it actually works. How are you *ready*?"

"You mean, how are *we* ready?"

"How are *we* ready ..." Ophelia looked down, wringing her hands. "How do you know how to grant wishes when we haven't even graduated yet?"

"I don't know." Leona shrugged again, this time more loosely. "Don't worry about it. We just are. I mean, obviously, right? I could go and grant a wish today if an orb chose me. I can't wait for my turn to come!"

She smiled at Ophelia but could see her enthusiasm wasn't shared. "And you know we do get extra lessons," she went on. "You know about that, don't you? Our special class, last period, each day?"

"Special class?" Ophelia looked up slowly, seeming slightly less anxious at last.

"It's a secret, too, of course," Leona added. "You can't actually tell anyone what it's for or anything about the things we learn. Which is why you might get *comments* from some Starlings ... like *Vivica*...." Leona growled the name bitterly through clenched teeth. "I'm just saying," she went on, "that 'officially'" – she made quotation marks with one hand – "as far as most Starlings know, it's a study group we go to."

"Oh, that's no problem for me," Ophelia said matter-of-factly. "I don't mind."

Leona looked at her. The little Starling appeared to be serious. "Well, that makes one of us, at least. Now, come on." She steered the freckled Starling towards the exit. "Let's get you moved into our dorm room. Our stuff's going to go together starmendously, I can tell. Hey, have you ever considered a makeover, by any star chance? I bet I could really do something with that hair...."

CHAPTER
5

The Star Darlings left Lady Stella's office and followed Leona and Ophelia to their room. They were all eager to get to know their new teammate better and answer whatever questions about their mission she might have.

When they reached the door, however, Leona herded them back on to the Cosmic Transporter and shooed them on their way.

"I need a little time *alone* with my new roommate, if you don't mind," she said.

"Moonbeams!" gasped Ophelia as they stepped through the door to the room. "Is that – is that a *stage*?"

"It sure is!" replied Leona, stepping on to the star-shaped golden platform in the centre of the room. Instantly, the floor lit up beneath her. Lights blinked in sequence round the base. The words *You're a star!* and *Leona!* took turns flashing behind her on a massive floor-to-ceiling holo-screen. Above, a disco ball covered with tiny star-shaped mirrors dangled from a crystal-studded chain. Stars of light danced over Ophelia and across the entire dorm room as it twirled like a rotating planet overhead.

"This is kind of the performance side of the room," explained Leona. "That's the dressing-room side, over there." She pointed past her bed, which was large and round and piled high with silk pillows and set on a pedestal. Around it hung a lacy curtain made of strings of twinkling lights. On the other side of the bed stood a full-length three-sided mirror. This, too, was framed by lights. An antique steamer trunk, overflowing with glamorous costumes in every possible shade of gold, stood open next to it.

"I guess they haven't had time to finish your side of the room yet," said Leona, turning to what used to be Scarlet's side, which was much more empty and much less interesting than before.

There now stood a plain solar-metal bed with a basic white moonfeather quilt and a single pillow of modest size. Each was trimmed in thin yellow ribbon, but

Leona had to squint to make that out. A simple chest
of drawers crouched in the corner as if it wasn't sure yet
that it wanted to stay.

"No, this is everything," said Ophelia.

Leona laughed, thinking it was a joke.

"Really, I don't need very much, you know."

Leona stared at her. Ophelia was serious. It took a
starmin for that fact to sink in.

"You mean you don't have a desk? Or a cosy chair?"
Leona gestured to her own desk and chair.

"No." Ophelia shook her head. "I just sit ... and
work ... on my bed."

"No holo-screen?"

"No. I use my Star-Zap."

"No *mirror*? Not even *one*?"

Ophelia shrugged apologetically.

"What about personal items?" She smiled,
remembering some of Scarlet's more 'interesting' things –
like her collection of globerbeem egg cases and her old
moonmoth-eaten top hat and black velvet cape.

"I have the Wish Pendant Lady Cordial gave me."

"Ooh, let me see!" Leona said.

Ophelia pulled up her plain yellow sleeve to
reveal a thick metal bracelet studded with yellow
star-shaped jewels.

"No way! I have a cuff, too!" exclaimed Leona. She showed Ophelia hers. "Startacular, no?" she said. "So ... what else?" she asked eagerly.

"What else?" Ophelia looked puzzled, so Leona explained by scooping up a cute little stuffed glion from her star-shaped beanbag chair. She tickled its chin and it purred. Then she ran her hand down its golden back. "Shine like the superstar you are!" it roared.

Leona hugged it close. "This," she said proudly, "is my Glionny. I've had him since I was a baby. He never says anything more than once."

"Ooh! May I see him?" Ophelia asked. She held her hands out and Leona passed him to her. "Hello, Glionny," she said, gingerly petting its star-studded mane.

"Glow like you mean it!" the toy purred.

"See?" Leona said. "You must have some special things from home, too...?" Her voice trailed off.

"No ... not really." Ophelia kept her head down.

"Where are you from, anyway?" Leona asked.

"I'm not exactly sure," said Ophelia. "But I've lived in Starland City for as long as I can remember."

"Okay, first lesson," said Leona. "Be proud of who you are – and that includes where you're from! That's one way to stand out. How amazing that you live in Starland City! I'm sure you've had so many incredible

adventures. Unlike me – who's from little old Flairfield."
She closed her eyes and pretended to snore. "Not that
I'm not proud of it," she said, her eyes popping open
again. "Naturally, I am. But listen to this: can you believe
I never once travelled farther than Flairfield Lake until
I came here, to Starling Academy? For real! I *know*!"
Leona groaned. "It's my parents. Ugh." She sighed.
"They're homebodies." She rolled her eyes. "What can
you do?" She smiled.

"All I can say," Leona went on, "is thank the lucky
stars I got into Starling Academy! Best day of my life –
so far. My parents made it *very* clear that if I didn't,
it would be Flairfield High for me. Even when I got
accepted, they asked me to think about giving up my
place and staying home. Can you *imagine*? Pass up this
chance? Has any Starling ever even done that before?
Not once – I asked. Not that wish granting is my one
goal in life, of course. Some Starlings could settle for
that, but not me. As you can probably tell, I have lots of
other talents." She nodded towards her stage. "I'm kind
of on my way to being a superstar, which is why Starland
City is *the* place for me! Still ..." Leona picked up a
holo-picture from her bedside table and blew each
member of her family a kiss. The people in the picture
each blew one back. "I do miss my family a lot. Aren't

they cute?" She turned the picture so Ophelia could see her two little sisters, her two older brothers, and, in the middle of them all, her mum and dad. "But enough about me! I want to know more about *you*!" Leona set the holo-picture down. "What do you like to do for fun?"

"I don't know...."

"Like music?"

"Well, um –"

"Want me to sing for you? Startastic idea!" Leona leaped back on to her stage and stuck a hand out towards a rack of gleaming golden microphones. A large one blinked, rose and floated to her. Leona grabbed it with both hands. "Let's turn the lights down, shall we?" she said with a nod. Immediately, the room dimmed. At the same time, two gold spotlights blinked on and converged, capturing her in their beams.

"Sit! Please!" Leona nodded towards her beanbag chair, and Ophelia obliged her by plopping down. Still cradling the stuffed glion in her arms, she tilted her chin up and smiled at Leona.

"Here. Want a gamma-chip cluster? My mum made them. They're soooo good!" Leona said, offering her one. "Just watch the flowers, if you would." She nodded towards a vase of delicate coral-coloured blossoms on the crystal table by the chair.

"Oh, they're so pretty. Where did they come from?" asked Ophelia.

"You know, I'm not really sure.... They just showed up one day – in all our rooms. It's a Star Darlings thing, we think. Maybe I should move them.... I'd hate for you to applaud and knock them over," she explained. "That's better for now, don't you think?"

The rest of the starday flew by – for Leona at least – as she performed her repertoire in its entirety ... plus a few encores for fun. She was frankly stunned when the landscape began to brighten outside her windows as the sun sank behind the Crystal Mountains and the moon began to rise. All of Starland, and Starlings, too, shone brighter in the evening, at lightfall, when the halo of energy surrounding the planet reached its most glorious peak.

Just then, Leona's Star-Zap flashed. Ophelia's did, as well.

"Dinner time? Already?" Leona let her mic drift back to its place on the stand and nodded the spotlights away. "Star apologies, Ophelia! We hardly talked about you at all! But don't worry! We will. We have plenty of time!" she assured her with a wink.

As Leona's eyes reopened, she noticed the flowers sitting in the corner of the room. She walked over and took them, pausing to smell them. It was hard not to; their fragrance was so very sweet. She sighed with pleasure, then turned to give her new roommate a chance to smell them ... but changed her mind suddenly.

"Well? Are you ready?" She sent the flowers to her dressing table and crossed her arms.

"Um ... yes." Ophelia jumped up from the chair and left Leona's stuffed glion on the seat.

"Hey! Careful!" Leona snapped. "Have a little respect for my things!"

"Star apologies!" said Ophelia. She hurried over to hand Leona her toy.

"Give me an *S*! Give me a *T*! Give me an *A*! Give me an *R*!" the glion roared while Ophelia's wide eyes began to fill with liquid glitter – otherwise known as Starling tears.

Instantly, Leona wished she could take her words back or at least tame them a bit. She sounded ... she sounded like Scarlet! *What's wrong with me?* she asked herself. She took a deep breath, let it out and tried to find a smile somewhere within. "It's fine," she finally growled. As she heard herself, she winced. "Let's just go to dinner."

As they left the room, Ophelia used her wrist to wipe her eye. "I was careless with your things, but I'll be more careful next time."

"And I guess I was a little hot-tempered," Leona admitted. "Star apologies. I think I was just hungry...." Leona gulped. *What's wrong with me?* she wondered.

CHAPTER
6

After dinner, Leona felt much, much better. And because of that, Ophelia did, too. Oddly, though, a delicious meal did not have the same effect on the other Star Darlings, who left the café seeming more irritated than ever before.

Breakfast the next morning wasn't much different, though some arguments had changed.

Sage and Cassie were bickering about holo-books. Cassie was certain that Sage had borrowed her copy of *Once Upon a Starry Night*.

"I didn't borrow it," Sage said.

"But I saw it in your hands," Cassie argued, her eyes blazing behind her star-shaped glasses.

"Okay, I picked it up, it's true," Sage admitted. "But it seemed kind of boring, so I put it back on your shelf."

Cassie's mouth opened in disbelief. "Boring? Are you serious? *Once Upon a Starry Night* is the best book ever. What's wrong with you?"

"What's wrong with *you*?" Sage retorted.

"And what's wrong with *you*?" Libby suddenly said, staring daggers at her roommate, Gemma.

"Who, me?" asked Gemma.

They had their own squabble going, about Gemma's housekeeping skills, which Libby deemed startacularly poor.

"That's what comes from living on a farm – messy seems normal," said Libby.

"That's not true," Gemma's older sister, Tessa, said. "We had to be very neat, but Gemma could never get the hang of it."

Tessa, meanwhile, had her own issues with Adora – specifically over their shared bouquet. Tessa thought the coral flowers looked much more pleasing on her green side of the room and clashed horribly with Adora's blue. Adora found the argument frankly absurd, however, as her holo-colour wheel clearly proved.

As they went on and on, Leona turned to Ophelia and rolled her eyes in a weary 'who cares?' way.

"Oh, my stars," Leona remarked to Ophelia as they left the table together, arm in arm. "Is it me, or did everyone wake up on the dark side of the moon today?"

"So they aren't always like that?" asked Ophelia.

"Oh, no," Leona said. "Well...." She rethought that. "Maybe, sort of, lately. But never as bad as today." She shrugged. "Lucky us, is all I can say. I was actually having the same problem with my old roommate until you took her place." She gave Ophelia's arm a happy squeeze. "We're like the perfect roommates! It's as if we've known each other forever already, don't you think?"

Ophelia smiled and nodded.

"It's a cosmic connection!" Leona continued. "For instance, I used to get mad at Scarlet for moving our flowers around, too. But with you I don't care. We're roommates. We *should* share!"

"What do you mean?" asked Ophelia. "Move what flowers? Where?"

"Our bouquet. You know." They emerged from the café and into a misty, sparkly rain. Leona closed her eyes and turned her face up, and Ophelia did the same. "Did you know they say that the rain on Wishworld doesn't even *sparkle*?" she asked Ophelia. "And that the lakes there *reflect* light but don't make any of their own?"

"Amazing," Ophelia said, nodding. "How do they get glitter into their star showers do you think?"

"Beats me." Leona shrugged, pulled out her Star-Zap and dialled up an energy-bubble umbrella for them both. "Anyway, I don't know where you put the flowers, but it's fine. I don't care," she went on.

"But I didn't move them," replied Ophelia.

"You didn't?" Leona turned to her just as the lights throughout the campus shifted spectrum, turning from warm white to rosy pink. "Time for first period already?" exclaimed Leona. "I guess I'd better get going to Wish Theory."

Ophelia was on her way to Wish Energy Manipulation. They arranged to meet up before Star Darlings class.

"I always thought it was strange, you and Tessa and Adora being in that special class," Ophelia told Leona as they made their way to the soundproof classroom where the secret class was held at the end of each school day. "And the others, too, I guess. You all seemed so smart in all your other classes. I mean, doesn't Adora win the Astro Science Fair every year?"

"So now you know," said Leona. "Lady Stella just made up that story to help keep our mission a secret. None of us likes it at all." Leona groaned. "But we're helping Starland, so it's worth it, I suppose."

Their special Star Darlings lesson that day was about young-Wisher theory and was taught by Professor Illumia Wickes, who led her class by tossing ideas into space to see how far they'd travel and how bright they'd grow.

"Star greetings, Ophelia!" she exclaimed as Ophelia and Leona entered the room. "I heard there had been a Star Darlings replacement, but I had no idea it would be you!" She whipped off her enormous star-shaped rose-tinted glasses and flashed a suprised but welcoming smile.

Her wraparound dress, Leona noticed, displayed a constantly shifting pattern of stars and moons. It would certainly have hypnotized anyone who stared at it too long.

"I see we're all here," Professor Illumia Wickes said as Leona and Ophelia took their seats and let them adjust to their height and weight, "so let's go ahead and get started. Our starhour always goes so fast! This starday, I want to give you a scenario and ask you what you'd do.... Say there's a young Wisher who wishes for a moonium dollars in Wishling currency –"

Libby's glittery arm shot up. "Trick question!" She grinned. "Money wishes fall into the 'greedy' category. We would never be called to grant a wish like that."

"Ahem. As I was saying," Professor Illumia Wickes continued, nodding at Libby, who lowered her hand to her lap, "a young Wisher wishes for a moonium dollars in Wishling currency, not for *herself*, but to pay for a new playground for her school, which doesn't have one. Now, tell me: how do you help?"

She gazed around the room as hands rose slowly.

"Yes? Sage?"

"Conjure a treasure? And help the Wisher find it?"

"Treasure ... interesting ..." The professor looked round the table again. "Any thoughts?"

Vega frowned and raised her hand.

"Yes, Vega? You don't agree?"

"It wouldn't work," Vega said.

"Oh? And why not?"

"Any currency or jewels or precious metals we conjured would glow or glitter on Wishworld and give themselves away."

"Ah, interesting point ..." Professor Illumia Wickes said, nodding. "Libby? Yes? Now you may speak."

"I *still* think it's a trick question," said Libby.

Gemma turned and asked, "Why?"

"Because as soon as you attach a price to a wish, doesn't it take the purity – and the truly good energy – away?"

"Ah, but does it?" asked Professor Illumia Wickes.

Leona spoke up. "I don't think so. It's the basic reflective property of wishing we learned last week. If the Wisher's heart is pure, then their wish has to be, too."

"Yes, but in a way, wouldn't that Wisher's wish be selfish?" Cassie asked. "I mean, the playground would be for her, as a student at that school...."

"Correct," said Tessa, "and yet it would be there long after she graduates and leaves the school.... Perhaps, though, you could nudge her away from the 'moonium dollar' wish towards a different one – but one that would have the same result?"

"Interesting!" Professor Illumia Wickes's smile lit up. "Such as ..."

"Such as the whole school community coming together to raise money," suggested Tessa.

"Oh, I know!" Astra exclaimed. "She could organize one of those '-athons' they do so much on Wishworld. A walkathon, or a jumpathon, or something like that!"

"Or a cake trade!" Gemma offered. "They're always doing those down there!"

"I think you mean a cake sale," said Professor Illumia Wickes. "But yes ... I like where this is going! Don't stop! Any more ideas?"

"How about a fashion show fundraiser?" said Adora. "Wishling garments are so dull, we know, but still it could be fun!"

"You know what would be the *most* fun?" said Leona. "A fundraising *concert*! And if it was my Wish Mission, I would sing – of course!" Energized, she turned to her new roommate. "What do you think, Ophelia?"

"I ... I...." Ophelia stared back at Leona blankly.

"Yes, Ophelia. What *do* you think? You've been very quiet!" Professor Illumia Wickes smiled. "Don't be shy just because you're new. Feel free to jump in here and tell us what *you* would do!"

"Um ... I ... uh ..."

"Go ahead," Leona urged.

"It's just ..." Ophelia winced as if her brain hurt. "It's just ... I'm a little confused. We didn't learn much about young Wishlings' wishes in our other Wish Theory class ... so I don't understand. And what exactly is a 'playground'?" She paused. "Is there, um, a vocabulary list I could get, by any chance?"

A few giggles circled the table along with a rainbow of raised eyebrows.

Gemma snorted and threw back her head. "What in the stars! I feel like we really are in a remedial class!" She laughed.

"Like you know *everything*," Libby muttered across the table to her roommate, not at all under her breath.

Gemma fired back a hot orange glare. "I know this: you think you're so neat and perfect, but you're not very good at making your bed."

"That's only because you crawl over it to move those flowers! Why can't you just leave them on my dressing table, where you know they look the best?"

Zwwooosh!

A ball of light appeared in the professor's hand and she tossed it to the back of the room. It skimmed right over their heads. The girls' mouths opened in disbelief.

"That's enough!" said Professor Illumia Wickes as the Star Darlings covered their heads. "So much negative energy!" She clucked and shook her head.

The light ball slowed and returned to her outstretched hand, where it dissolved into a shimmering shower, spark by spark.

"Star apologies," said Libby.

"Yes, star apologies." Gemma looked down.

"Star apologies accepted, but all this bickering has got to stop. Now ..." She scanned her holo-notes. "I'd like to spend the rest of the class on this idea of young wishful thinking, so if you'd all get out your Star-Zaps, please. Feel free to record my lecture so you can absorb it in your sleep...."

"Ophelia! Wait!" Leona hurried after Ophelia, who was the first Starling out of the door. "Don't listen to Gemma," she said, linking her arm with Ophelia's. "Every Starling knows she has the biggest mouth in school."

"But she's right," said Ophelia as they rode the Cosmic Transporter out of the front door of the school. "I'm so far behind the rest of you. I don't know where to begin to catch up! And it's not just that. I've seen some of the things the other Star Darlings – and you – can do with energy, and I'm nowhere even close...."

"You'll get there!" Leona tried to reassure her. "It might take some time, but you will!"

"But how? Do you know, when Lady Cordial first called me into her office, I thought I was being expelled. Do you know I got a D on my Wishworld Relations exam last week?"

"Really?" said Leona, stunned. D, for *Dim*, was the lowest grade a Starling could get.

"And it's not only that. You're so *special*! And the other Star Darlings, too. I don't fit in at all, and I don't see how I ever will...."

"Come on." Leona took a sharp right, on to a path towards the edge of the campus.

"Where are we going?" Ophelia asked.

Leona pointed towards a thick grove of pink ozziefruit trees just past the campus border. It was her favourite place to walk and sing and think. "A few berries?" She winked at Ophelia. "They make everything better, don't you agree?"

As soon as the Cosmic Transporter reached the orchard, Leona and Ophelia stepped off and walked between rows of tall pink-leaved trees heavy with ripe indigo fruit. Leona reached out and picked a berry for Ophelia and another one for herself. Instantly, two new fruits grew in their places, just as big and juicy and blue.

"Shall we sit?" Leona asked, settling in the grass at the base of the fragrant tree. As Ophelia sank beside her, Leona took a bite out of her ozziefruit. "Mmm!" Leona said as she chewed and dabbed at a stream of blue juice dribbling down her chin.

Ophelia smiled.

"See? I knew these would make you feel better. And you haven't even eaten one yet."

"It's your mouth ..." Ophelia said, pointing.

"What?" Leona glanced down at blue ozziefruit-juice stains on her fingers. "Oh, no!" She laughed. "Are my lips blue?" She shrugged. "Who cares? It's worth it! See? I'm not that special after all!"

Just above them, a delicate 12-legged rainbow-orb spider was busy weaving her star-shaped web. The star-silk stretched between the branches like shiny tinsel, flashing wherever the sunlight found it.

"Did you feel this way at first?" Ophelia asked Leona. "Like you didn't know why you were picked?"

Leona almost answered "Sure", but then she realized that wasn't true. In fact, she remembered clearly how right being chosen had felt. *Of course, I'm a Star Darling!* she'd thought when Lady Stella assembled them the first day. *And I'm going to be the best!*

"Don't worry," she told Ophelia instead. "It's going to get easier. Use your Mirror Mantra! It always helps me."

"Mirror Mantra?" said Ophelia.

"Yes, you know – the words you recite when you need strength or reassurance. You can use it with your Wisher, too."

Ophelia looked at her blankly. "Um, I don't know ... I guess I haven't got one yet."

"No? That's odd. Well, I'm sure you will. This is mine: 'You are a star. Light up the world.'" Leona grinned proudly. "Nice, right? When you say it without a mirror, it makes you feel good and positive. When you say it on Wishworld in front of a mirror, you can see yourself with your Starland glow."

"Do you think I could use yours? Until I get mine?"

Leona's eyes brightened. "Sure! Knock your stars out!"

Then, suddenly, both their Star-Zaps flashed.

"Ooh! What's going on?" Ophelia looked down as hers began to vibrate wildly – much more strongly than it did for a normal alert.

Leona read the screen, already knowing what it would say. "Another Wish Orb's been identified!" she told Ophelia. "Come on! We need to get to Lady Stella's office ASAS – as soon as starpossible!"

"Not to the Wish-House?" said Ophelia, scrambling to her feet.

"The Wish-House is for *regular* wishes," said Leona. "We have a special, secret one – way under Halo Hall – for no other wishes, just ours!" She quickly grabbed a handful of berries. "For energy!" she said. "After all, who knows? The Wish Orb might belong to one of us!"

CHAPTER
7

Soon Leona, Ophelia and the other Star Darlings stood in a circle round the grass-covered platform from which a Wish Orb would soon reveal itself.

Leona looked up and saw clouds drifting slowly across the blue sky. As usual, she had to remind herself that they were underground and not in Starland City Park.

"Are you ready, Star Darlings?" asked Lady Stella, raising her arms to begin the process of the Wish Orb Reveal.

Leona knew she was ready. She gazed around and could see that the others were as well – everyone, that is, but poor Ophelia, who looked as if she'd eaten *way* too much zoomberry cake and was about to lose it all. Cassie didn't look very confident, either.

Lady Stella clapped once and the room fell dark, save for one pure white beam of light shining down on the platform, which slowly opened up, revealing a brilliant orb. It hovered in the air and then did something different: it started to race round the circle, zooming up to each Star Darling for a split second and then zipping across the circle towards another. Leona's eyes lit up each time it approached her, and her smile faded each time it zipped away. She closed her eyes in frustration.

"Leona!" someone shouted.

She opened her eyes. The beautiful, tantalizing orb floated in the air in front of her.

She reached out and the orb fitted in her palm perfectly. She felt a wave of pure bliss as she gazed down at it.

"Congratulations, Leona," said Lady Stella, pressing her palms together and bowing over them.

"How long till I go?" Leona asked. "Tomorrow morning? Afternoon?"

"Actually...." The headmistress stood over the Wish Orb and studied it. "I do believe that in the case of this wish, there isn't a starmin to lose. As you know, a Wish Orb will stay fresh and healthy as long as the Wisher keeps wishing on the wish ... but if they begin to forget ... or change their mind ... their Wish Orb will lose its glow and fade away."

"Is that what's happening?"

"It certainly appears so," said Lady Stella. "The glow is already fading, I'm afraid. This wish needs granting very soon...."

"Then what are we waiting for?" said Leona. "All I really need is my Wish Pendant, right? Then I can go and catch a shooting star!"

From the underground Wish-House, Leona followed Lady Stella out of the Star Caves. After a brief stop in the headmistress's office for a quick refresher on the features she'd need to use on her Star-Zap when she got to Wishworld, Leona raced back to her room to be sure she had everything she needed.

Back in Halo Hall, she boarded the Flash Vertical Mover, and in mere starsecs she was whisked into the sky. Lady Stella and the rest of the Star Darlings were there to see her off, all wearing their Safety Star Glasses. Leona hugged the Star Darlings goodbye, leaving Ophelia with an extra-strong, supportive squeeze.

"Remember what I told you. This is all strange and new right now, but it's going to get easier every starday! You're going to be a great Star Darling, Ophelia! Just hang in there and believe in yourself! Promise you'll try my Mirror Mantra. Remember how it goes?"

Ophelia took a hopeful breath. "'You are a star. Light up the world.'"

"Exactly! You've got it!"

Lady Stella gave Leona some last-minute advice. "Focus on your mission. Be sure you don't get caught up in the excitement of being on Wishworld," she reminded Leona. "And be sure to discover your Wisher's true wish – not the wish you think she may have made."

Lady Cordial gave Leona her rucksack with the stuffed star-shaped keychain and wished her luck.

On the Special Star Darling Wishworld Surveillance Deck, Star Wranglers were already waiting with lassos made of wish energy to harness Leona to the next shooting star, which came before she even had time to think *Am I ready?* or *Should I have brought a microphone?* The next thing Leona knew, she was strapped to the star and hurtling through space like a golden meteor.

It was beautiful! The colours were endless – like a giant box of cray-osmic crayons times a hydrong. Leona had to force herself to focus on her mission like Lady Stella had said, and to use the precious starmins she had to prepare for what was to come. It was hard, though, not to simply gaze around, enjoying a view of the universe that only a few Starlings ever got to see.

Fortunately, she had her Star-Zap to alert her when it was time to commence her appearance change. By then, she had entered Wishworld's atmosphere and could see the shapes of the continents below. She hurried to pull up the Wishworld Outfit Selector on her Star-Zap and choose something Wishlingy to wear. Then she closed her eyes, placed her hand over her golden cuff, and recited the body-transforming lines: "Star light, star bright, the first star I see tonight: I wish I may, I wish I might, have the wish I wish tonight." A soothing warmth spread through her body, and she envisioned what she'd look like on Wishworld – hair that was light brown instead of gold, and skin that was still honey brown but shimmerless and dull. She opened her eyes slowly to see if the mantra had worked.

"Starmendous!" she said out loud, shaking the stars loose from her hair.

Her Star-Zap flashed: PREPARE FOR LANDING. And Leona did, once more closing her eyes. She braced for a jolt, but she was far from ready for the icy-cold splash she got instead.

"*Argh!*" she wailed, opening her eyes to find herself in the middle of a wide blue tree-lined lake.

She grabbed the star and swam to shore as fast as she could, grateful for her water ballet lessons in

Luminous Lake. Unfortunately, while all bodies of water on Starland instantly adjusted to any temperature a swimmer might desire – from hot-tub warm to refreshingly cool – the water in this Wishworld lake was most *undesirably* ice-cold.

Leona reached the bank and climbed out, shivering, only to feel colder when her wet skin met the air. Without her natural star energy glow and shimmer, she had no way to keep off the chill. But she did have a Star-Zap – fortunately – which meant a whole wardrobe of dry clothes. She quickly pulled it out and dialled up the warmest outfit she could find: a butter-soft, long-sleeved gold sweater with a chenille star appliquéd on the chest, a pair of brown leggings flecked with gold and cosy fleece-lined boots covered with tiny shiny gold sequins.

Then she took a starmin to make a mental note, which would be recorded in her Cyber Journal when she pressed a button on her Star-Zap.

Mission 3, Wishworld Observation #1: Wishworld water is cold. Recommend including a drying feature in future Star Darlings' Star-Zaps.

Leona shook the water off her star and folded it up. She checked her image in her Star-Zap and was pleased – with the outfit, at least. Her hair, on the other hand, was dripping wet. On Starland, of course, this never happened. Hair looked exactly the same dry or wet. Leona wished she knew what Wishlings did with their hair in these situations, but the subject had never come up in class. All she could do was give it a shake and hope it dried by itself.

Most important, she knew, was to find her Wisher, and she turned once more to her Star-Zap for that. "Take me to the Wisher I've come to help," she said, holding the Star-Zap out to see where it would lead. *Before my Wisher forgets her wish*, she thought, *or somehow changes her mind*.

Directions appeared on the holo-screen and Leona followed them away from the lake and through the trees. Pine trees. Leona recognized them from a holo-picture in the Wishworld Relations classroom; only in that picture, the trees were frosted with plain white Wishworld snow. On Starland they had snow, as well, but the flakes were all different colours and looked like confetti when they fell. Leona remembered thinking how much fun it would be, just once, to have one-colour snow. She would, of course, have picked gold.

Before too long, the directions led her out of the woods and into the sun, on to a lush green Wishworld lawn. Leona paused to let the warm rays sink in, then continued down a lane to a tall, dull-black yet impressively detailed iron fence similar to the one that ran around Starling Academy. She noticed words at the top and read them: "'Havisham Academy – Boarding School for Girls'. Havisham Academy … oh!" gasped Leona. "This must be the place!" Perhaps it was even a school for special Wishlings, like Starling Academy was for Starlings.

Much like at Starling Academy, a long driveway led through the gate and was lined with stately broad-limbed trees. Unlike along Starling Academy's Constellation Lane, though, the leaves along this Wishworld road remained a single colour – green. The drive circled at the end, where it reached a wide rectangular building made of rough reddish bricks. Leafy green ropes grew up the walls, all the way to the slate roof.

Leona was checking her Star-Zap again to see if it might inform her that her Wisher was inside when all of sudden, without any warning, the doors flew open and a flood of young female Wishlings poured out. And they weren't just coming from that one building, Leona soon realized, but from similar-looking structures all around. Some kept to the paths that criss-crossed the well-trimmed lawns, and some hiked across the grass. Leona froze, fearing one of the kids might run over her if she kept moving.

"Look out!"

It almost happened anyway. A line of three girls stopped short just in front of her, forcing Leona to stumble back.

"Oh, sorry," one said.

"You probably shouldn't stand here."

"Yeah, not when classes finish, at least."

"Are you looking for someone?" the first girl asked.

"Who, me?" *If they only knew*, Leona thought. "Um, actually, I go here!"

"You *do*?" Two girls raised their eyebrows. The third eyed Leona from head to toe. "Then why aren't you wearing a uniform?"

"A what?" Leona said.

The third girl nodded towards her outfit, then gave a quick chin bob to each of her friends. That's when Leona noticed for the first time that they – and every other girl in sight – were all dressed exactly alike: black shoes, tall white socks folded just below the knee, crisp white shirts with plain white buttons in a row all down the front, red-and-blue-striped strips of fabric tied in knots round their necks, tartan skirts with a large decorative pin, and, finally, boxy storm-grey blazers with shield-shaped patches attached to pockets on their chests.

"Right. A uniform." Leona remembered now. They had learned about those in class. Only, she thought those were clothes *adult* Wishlings wore for some of their special jobs, like putting out fires or fighting crime – things that on Starland never needed to be done. And then there were the uniforms adult Wishlings wore when they played young Wishling games in front of crowds. But to school? Leona must have somehow missed that lesson. Or laughed it off as a joke.

"So ... this is the uniform ... today?" Her finger jumped from girl to girl. "And tomorrow, I guess, you wear a different one? Is there, by any chance, a *gold* day?"

The girls' faces wrinkled into different patterns of confusion.

"We wear this *every* day. I thought you went here," one of them said.

"I do...."

Every day? thought Leona. If she'd been on Starland, she'd surely have lost her glow.

"But I'm new ... I just arrived...." Leona forced herself to add a smile, but it was hard to make it stay. The image of *her* in *that* made her want to cry instead.

"Oh! So you're probably looking for the headmistress," said the first girl. "She'll give you a uniform and show you to your room." She pointed to the door they'd just come out of. "In there. First door on the left."

"Star salu– oh, I mean, thanks," said Leona. She waved and watched the girls walk off. Then she turned and headed in to get her ... *gulp* ... school uniform.

Mission 3, Wishworld Observation #2: Warning! Be prepared: choice of Wishling wardrobe is not guaranteed.

Finding the headmistress was easy, as was convincing her that Leona was enrolled in her school. The mind-control techniques Sage and Libby had taught Leona and the others worked beautifully on her. Almost instantly, Leona was being given a room assignment, a class timetable, and, of course, a uniform while the headmistress remarked on the sudden scent of baking brownies and paused now and then to lick her lips. She told Leona her room number and handed her a key. Leona politely refused her offer to show her the way. She wanted to find her Wisher immediately.

From there, Leona slipped into the toilets and quickly changed. She was more eager than ever to get on with her mission (and back to her wardrobe on Starland) as soon as possible.

"Now, where is my Wisher?" She checked to see if her Star-Zap had any further instructions to give. "*Argh!*" she cried as she suddenly noticed a Wishling girl standing right there.

Leona reeled back in surprise. "You scared me –" she started. Then she realized the pretty, curly-haired Wishling was saying the same thing.

"*Starf!*" she said to her reflection in the mirror above the sink. She knew she was supposed to look like a real Wishling ... but still, it was hard to accept! She fluffed her hair, which had dried out fairly well. "You are a star," she said. "Light up the world!" Her sparkly self stared back at her. And a surge of energy boosted her confidence. And with that, she opened the toilet door and charged into the hall.

According to the headmistress, classes were over for the day. The hall, therefore, was empty, and Leona's footsteps echoed as her stiff new loafers clip-clopped across the floor.

Leona figured she'd head back outside and hope her Star-Zap directed her from there. She paused, though, as she passed a bulletin board, and did a double take. If there were two words that could catch her eye, they were the ones at the top of the pale pink flyer pinned between a wonky sign about a yearbook meeting and another about a term in somewhere called Spain.

Leona read the two words at the top of the pink flyer out loud: "'Talent show'."

A happy tingle made its way up her spine as she eagerly read on: "'Auditions today from five to nine pm in Hawthorne Auditorium.'"

Of course! she thought. *That's got to be where I'll find my Wisher!* She glanced up at the clock above the bulletin board. The time was 4.45pm. *Here I come, whoever you are!* she thought as she turned and ran, loafers clippety-clapping, to find the auditorium.

CHAPTER
8

Hawthorne Auditorium turned out to be easy to find. The building took up most of the north end of the quad.

Leona was less sure, though, once she skipped up the steps and slipped through the front doors. There wasn't much to see: just a narrow lobby with framed posters in rows along the walls, two pairs of doors, and one wide-eyed grown-up Wishling waving a clipboard.

"Who are you? And how did you do that?"

"Excuse me?" Leona said. She covered her Wish Pendant with her hand. What exactly had she done? Something un-Wishlingish, she guessed.

"How did you open those doors like that and walk right through?"

"Uh...." Leona looked back at the doors behind her. "Isn't that how all doors work?" She knew Wishworld was different ... but weren't all doors simply doors?

"But you didn't push! And they're not automatic. Your hands were down at your sides the whole time...." The woman reached out and yanked hard on the door handle to open it. "See? They don't just open. They're heavy. They stick."

Leona gulped. She understood. She'd been so focused on finding her Wisher she'd forgotten to be careful not to let her energy work for her.

Mission 3, Wishworld Observation #3: When on Wishworld, never use energy when you can use your hands. Not only will you conserve energy, you'll avoid embarrassing questions.

"Um ... you are absolutely right," she told the woman, gazing deep into her eyes. "Those doors are very heavy. That's why I pushed them very hard – with my hands. And that's how I got in."

The woman's baffled scowl softened into a friendly, vaguely hungry grin. "You pushed them very hard with your hands," she repeated. "That's how you got in. Mmm. Warm apple pie." She sighed. "I could use a piece right now."

Leona sighed, too. *That was pretty easy. Now, back to the mission at hand.* "I'm here for the auditions. Where are they exactly?" she asked.

"You're here for the auditions. Of course." The woman nodded. "They're in the auditorium, just through there." She aimed a pen at a pair of double doors. "And your name is...?" she asked.

"Um, Leona ... I'm new.... I sing!" she added before she could think to stop. "Uh, but I'm really just here to watch," she went on quickly. "If that's okay, of course."

"To watch?" The woman looked up. Her face was still calm and sweet and stiff. "That's okay, of course. I was just on my way in myself. I'm Ms Frasier, the music director. I'm in charge of the auditions." She shifted her clipboard and held out her hand.

"Really? Nice to meet you!" Leona shook it heartily. "Here!" She ran to the doors to the auditorium. "Let me get the door for you, Ms Frasier. With my hands, of course!"

Once they were inside, it all made sense to Leona. *Now, this is more like it!* she thought.

Her gaze moved down the aisle, along the rows of seats, and up on to the empty stage. No, it wasn't star shaped, and the curtains, unfortunately, were rust-coloured, with no neon twinkle at all. Still, it was all Leona could do not to run up there, grab the mic, and belt out a rocking song.

But no, this was not the time. She had to remind herself of that twice. With luck, that would come soon enough, but Leona still had to find her Wisher. Then would come the hardest part of all: identifying the Wisher's wish.

She dragged her eyes from the stage and began to scan the auditioners. She saw Ms Frasier doing the same.

"Okay, people! Let's do this!" the music teacher shouted as she marched down the aisle towards the first row of seats. "We have a long list of auditions to get through here, so I want you ready when I call your name!"

Leona quickly counted. There were 48 girls in the auditorium, most scattered among the seats. Two sat at the end of the row right next to her. She decided to start with them.

"Hi," she said.

The first girl turned. It looked like she held a small child on her lap. A strange, tiny little kid.

The friend turned as well, stiffly. "Hi, hello there!" she declared.

Leona jumped back.

"Oh, my stars!" she gasped.

The first girl dissolved into laughter while her small friend stared off into space.

"What?" said Leona. "What's so funny?"

"Nothing," said the girl, laughing. She covered her mouth with her free hand. "It's just that you look really startled by Dolly. Like you thought she was a real girl."

Leona didn't know what to say. She did know that her Wish Pendant did not show this was her Wisher, so she smiled and slowly backed away.

"Excuse us, we're trying to rehearse here," said a sharp voice, which made Leona spin round.

"Oh, sorry!" She smiled at the three girls. "What's your talent?" she inquired.

They all looked at her and then at each other's matching shorts and leotards.

"Dance," one said, swinging her hip to meet her hand.

Another nodded. "Jazz."

"Wait, Talia, I thought it was modern," the third one said, frowning.

"Whatever, Adeline." The first girl, Talia, rolled her eyes back to Leona and lifted one cheek in a half grin. "What's *your* talent?" she asked. "Staring? Good one, right, Kasey?"

"Ha!" Kasey laughed.

"Can you do that as a talent?" asked Adeline.

"It was a joke," explained Talia. She was their leader, Leona guessed.

Leona wondered if maybe these girls didn't want to be mean and wished they weren't that way. She checked her Wish Pendant, but it was barely glowing. None of the girls was her Wisher. Too bad. That would have been such a great wish to grant, helping one of them change into a better person.

"First up! Make-a-Move!" said the music teacher.

"Omigosh, Talia! We're first!" Kasey squealed.

"First?" Adeline blanched.

"First is good!" Talia declared. "Then we can get out of here and eat, and we don't have to sit through all these weirdos, like Hannah and her creepy dummy."

She nodded towards the girl with the little stiff friend as she said that. The other girls giggled behind their hands.

"Come on, let's go!" Talia went on, dragging her dance mates down the aisle.

"Good luck," Leona told them.

"Thanks," Adeline said.

Talia tossed her ponytail. "Who needs luck when you have talent? But yeah ..." She snorted. "Thanks, lemonhead."

Leona watched them head towards the stage, wishing she could take her 'good luck' back. She had no idea what a lemonhead was, but it didn't sound like a compliment. Still, she couldn't take things on Wishworld personally.

She had to remind herself of that. She was there on a mission, and it was way too important to let silly names distract her from that.

And besides, she thought, she had more talent in her little finger than those three Make-a-Moves combined.

Anyway ... Leona sighed and turned at a sound behind her. A girl stood in the back of the theatre, blinking nervously, looking as if she was afraid the auditorium would swallow her. Leona walked up to the girl, and feeling her wrist tingle, she looked down at her Wish Pendant. She was nearly blinded by its glow.

"Hi. My name's Leona. What's yours?"

"Er ... Lily," the girl said, then gulped. She stared at the floor.

"Lily!" Leona nodded. "That's a pretty name! So ... Lily ... are you here to audition for this thing?"

Her head still down, the girl nodded.

Awesome! Leona thought. There was only one wish this Wisher could have: to win this talent show!

"So what's your talent?" she asked the girl. "Or should I say *which* talent do you want to perform?"

The girl took a long, deep breath and held it. "Singing," she said, exhaling at last.

"Really?" Leona could hardly contain her excitement. This was going to be the best mission ever!

Meanwhile, music had started and so had Make-a-Move's routine. Leona didn't see too much talent in their dancing, yet she couldn't tear her eyes away. They did what they did with such self-confidence – just like Leona, in a way.

Even Lily looked up and watched them as most of the audience started to clap. Their dance involved a lot of rolling hips and stomping feet and crossing arms and pumping fists, along with a good bit of running in place and making fierce faces that featured curled lips.

"Wow," said Leona as the dancers finally dropped to their knees at the end. "They know how to get your attention. You have to admit that, I guess."

Onstage, the girls hugged and high-fived. Then they linked arms and took a bow. This was followed by another bow, and another –

"Okay, thank you, Make-a-Move," Ms Frasier shouted. "Really, thank you. But let's keep it moving. We've got a long list here. Okay ... who's next? Let's see.... Lily. *Lily!*" she shouted. "It's your turn!"

"Hey, that's you!" exclaimed Leona. She turned back to cheer on her Wisher, only to find that her Wisher was gone. "Wait! Lily!" she called to the closing door. "You can't go now! It's your turn!"

She slipped through the door, too, and caught Lily in the lobby, just about to go outside. "Lily! Ms Frasier just called your name! You're up! It's your turn to get up there and shine!"

But Lily just stood there, her head shaking back and forth, her mouth clamped firmly shut. It took Leona a starsec to finally realize that her Wisher had stage fright.

Just then, Make-a-Move burst out of the theatre and into the lobby.

"Omigosh! *Lily Fisher!*" Talia covered her mouth. "Are *you* the Lily Ms Frasier's calling? Please tell me you're not really going to audition."

"Of course she's going to!" declared Leona. No one was talking to her Wisher that way! "You auditioned," she reminded Talia, "so why shouldn't she?"

"Uh, yeah," Talia said, "and we have *talent*. And since this is a talent show, that's kind of something that you need."

She laughed, and so did Kasey. Their friend Adeline, however, shrugged.

"I don't know," she said. "Haven't you heard her sing in chorus? If I were her, I might try out. She's really pretty good."

At this, both Talia and Kasey turned to their friend and glared.

Lily, though, didn't seem to hear her. She'd already opened the door to the quad and was halfway through it.

Leona brushed past the dance group to follow her, scowling at Talia as she did. "Just so you know, your routine was fine, but you were totally off beat." She was so mad she nearly forgot to open the doors like a Wishling *again*. They were already starting to open by the time she remembered and lifted her hands.

Leona ran outside and spotted Lily heading down a brick path towards a building just beyond the quad.

"Hey!" she panted, catching up. "Don't listen to them. I'm sure you can sing! Let's go back so we – I mean *you*; of course, I mean you – so *you* can audition. Come on!"

Lily slowed down but kept walking, her eyes fixed on the ground. "I'm not going to audition," she said softly.

"But ... but I thought ... I thought you wanted to," Leona said, confused.

Lily shook her head. "No," she said very definitely. "I was just kidding when I said that. I never really wanted to. It was a joke, signing up. I don't belong in any talent show." She looked up at last as they reached a long brick building. Solemnly, she opened the door. "After you," she told Leona, forcing a smile and waving Leona past her.

"What's this place?" asked Leona. Her nose twitched at the rush of new smells. They were heavy and strange and thick.

Lily looked at her oddly. "It's the dining hall."

"Really?" Leona looked around. *Ah, yes, of course.* She spotted the queue of girls taking trays and sliding them down a silver track, past a line of older Wishlings in paper aprons and gauzy hair nets.

"So, what, are you new here?" asked Lily, gazing more closely at her.

"Um ... yes." Leona quickly nodded. "In fact, I just got here today."

"Are you a sophomore, too?"

"Um ... sure." Leona could be a sophomore, she guessed – whatever a sophomore was.

"Well, the food's pretty good. Except for the meatballs," said Lily. "Here, take a tray. And there's always the salad bar, and pasta. And we just got a frozen yogurt machine, but it keeps breaking, I'm afraid."

"Oh? That's too bad...." A thought suddenly popped into Leona's head. "I bet you wish it would get fixed."

Lily shrugged. "Yeah, I guess.... But I'm lactose intolerant, so I don't care that much, I guess."

She seemed to care, however, because her face suddenly went pale. She'd been looking at Leona, but her eyes had shifted to something in the distance, past Leona. Leona turned and saw an older girl approaching, shaking her head.

"So." The girl crossed her arms. "Guess what I just heard."

Lily sucked in her lips. Her ears and neck flushed.

"You bailed on the talent show audition. Why are you always such a wimp?"

Lily's mouth fell open, but nothing came out except a meek breath.

"Excuse me!" huffed Leona, but the older girl was already walking away. "Honestly!" said Leona. "Who does that girl think she is?"

Lily swallowed, sniffed, and found her voice. "She's my big sister," she explained.

CHAPTER
9

Leona was speechless – for a starsec. But a starsec was all it took for Lily to drop her tray back on the pile and flee the dining hall.

Leona was tempted to follow her again, but she wasn't sure that she should. She had a limited amount of time to help grant Lily's wish, yet what did Professor Eugenia Bright always say? "Haste makes waste." *Think things through before you act*, in other words.

Plus, Leona's stomach was growling. Better to see what this Wishworld cafeteria had to offer, she thought, and restore her energy. One thing was for sure, though: she'd be eating by herself. She knew there were plenty of nice Wishlings on Wishworld – or so other Starlings had said – but the girls at Havisham Academy so far seemed pretty unpleasant.

Leona pushed her tray – with her hands – along the counter briskly, taking a little bit of everything. Everything, that is, but the stuff labelled 'meatballs', as Lily had warned her. When she saw it, it was easy to skip. She saw the wedges labelled 'pizza' and remembered what Libby had said about it – delicious! She took two.

"Wow, you must be hungry," said someone behind her.

Leona closed her eyes and sighed. *Starf,* she thought. Just what she needed. Yet another Wishling giving her a hard time.

She glanced over her shoulder to see the smiling face of one of the girls who'd almost run into her when she'd first arrived. "But you skipped the meatballs. Smart. I see you got a uniform."

Leona nodded.

"Cool! Welcome! My name's Calley. Want to sit with us?" She pointed to some girls already sitting at a table nearby. Two were the other girls she'd met in the courtyard. They all waved back and smiled.

"Um ... yeah," said Leona. "Sure." It was still sinking in, the fact that the girl was being nice. Leona supposed she hadn't been so mean at first, either, now that she thought about it.

"What do you want to drink?" asked the girl as they reached the drinks counter. She took two plastic tumblers and offered Leona one.

"Um...." Leona could have used a nice cup of Zing, but that would have to wait until her Starland return. She remembered the icy-cold drink described as the perfect sweet-sour combination from Introduction to Wishworld.

"Do you have something here called ... lemonade, I think?"

Calley's smile grew even wider. "Lemonade?" she said.

"Yes!" Leona grinned. "That's it!"

Calley pointed to a machine with a shiny picture of some kind of oblong bright yellow fruit on it.

Leona read the word splashed across the bottom. "No way! Lemonade! You *do* have it! This is super startastic!" she exclaimed.

Leona filled her cup, tasted it, and then gulped most of it down and filled her cup once again. It was just as delicious as they said. Much happier than she'd been before, she followed Calley to her friends' table.

Each girl introduced herself politely.

"What year are you?" a girl named Sophia, asked.

"Um...." Leona tried to remember. "A starmore, I think."

"A what?" The girl wrinkled her nose and frowned.

Leona tried again. "A softstar?"

"Do you mean 'sophomore'?" asked a dark-haired girl named Maya.

"Right!" said Leona. "That's it."

"Are you an exchange student?" Calley asked.

"Why ... yes! Yes, I am! How'd you know?"

"We can just tell." Calley smiled.

"Where are you from?" Sophia asked.

"Where am I from...." Leona tried to recall Wishworld places they'd learned, but her mind had become a black hole. *Wait!* She remembered the sign on the bulletin board about what looked like a beautiful place. "Spain!" she said, a little more loudly than she needed to, perhaps.

"Wow," said Maya, looking impressed. "Your English is really good!"

"Uh ... thanks." It was time to change the subject. "Sooooo ... are any of you auditioning for the talent show?" she asked.

"No."

"No way."

They all shook their heads.

Calley even made a face as if she might get sick. "I auditioned last year, but I never will again."

"Why not?" Leona asked.

"Talia and her friends. They've won for the last two years. And they're not even all that good."

"No," Sophia helped her explain, "but what they are is super mean, so that girls either quit and drop out or get too nervous to do their best."

"Someone should stand up to them," said Leona.

"You're right." They all agreed.

"You're welcome to try." Calley nodded at her, but she looked doubtful of Leona's success.

Not Leona, though. Her thoughts were orbiting, working to make a plan. After all, if Lily's wish was going to come true in time, Leona might have to be the one to make it happen.

After they'd eaten, the girls had to head to the library to do their homework, so Leona said goodbye. She had her own work to do, and she knew that if she didn't find Lily and get her to those auditions before they ended at nine o'clock, making her Wisher's wish come true would be impossible.

She decided to go and check out her new dorm room. She fished the key out of her pocket. Room 113. She found the building – Auburn Hall – and stepped inside. She paused in front of the door, then unlocked it.

Leona heard the sound of a tap turning on through the bathroom door. Her roommate was taking one of those water showers, she guessed. Another reason she should go.

Leona turned to enter the hall, but then something made her stop. It was another sound: a voice – her roommate's, apparently – singing a sad, sweet song.

Wow ... Leona moved to her bed and stretched out on it to listen better. The girl was really good, and with every verse her voice grew even stronger and clearer and more sure of itself. The song was catchy and easy to follow, and Leona found herself singing along. She soon stopped, though, and sat back and listened, eyes closed, as the girl hit heavenly notes Leona knew she never would. *If only other Starlings could hear this*, she thought. *Wait!* She realized they could! She pulled out her Star-Zap, held it up, and began to record.

Then the shower stopped, and, unfortunately, so did the song. A starmin later, the bathroom door opened.

"*Lily?*" Leona gasped the moment she saw her. She recognized her Wisher at once even with her wet hair and music-note pyjamas.

"*Argh!*" Lily jumped back. "You scared me! What are you doing here?" She looked confused.

"Actually – I'm your new roommate," Leona told her. "They put me here this afternoon. Some coincidence, huh? I sing, and so do you!" She grinned. "And wow! You're really good!"

Lily was clearly trying not to smile at Leona's compliment, but she couldn't contain her grin. "I didn't know anyone could hear me," she explained.

"Oh, don't apologize! Not for a second!" said Leona. "I believe in singing as loud as you can. I also believe that a voice like yours should be heard. Honestly, it's a gift you were born to share!"

"Thanks." Lily blushed. "But I'm not *that* good."

"Um, yeah," said Leona. "You are. And you are crazy not to enter that talent show. So hurry, come on, let's go!"

At that, Lily started shaking her head. Her smile faded and her blush disappeared.

"What's wrong?"

"I'm not going to audition," said Lily.

"But why not? You're so good! You'll win!"

"That's not what those girls said...."

"Yeah, and I hear they say that to everyone else, too. Honestly, it's time for someone to step up and show them they can't keep using bullying to win."

"Yeah, well, someone else will have to show them. I just can't sing in front of other people, not all by myself."

"Of course you can!" Leona insisted.

"No, I can't," said Lily, stubbornly shaking her towel-wrapped head.

"Have you tried?" asked Leona.

"No ... not really."

"Exactly! So you have no idea! In fact, if you'd tried, you'd know that all by yourself is the best way in the universe to sing!" Leona declared.

"I don't know about that...." Lily laughed, but she couldn't argue. Leona could tell that her mind was beginning to change. *And not a starmin too soon*, Leona realized as she glanced at the clock by the bed. It was already 8.55pm. They only had five minutes left!

"So will you audition?" asked Leona. "I'll go with you – for moral support...." She reached out and took Lily's hands.

"Oh!"

Leona could feel Lily shiver. "Oops. Star ap– I mean, sorry!" Leona said, dropping Lily's hands.

"That's okay...." Lily rubbed her palms and wiggled her fingers. "There's a lot of static in the air, I guess." Then she smiled broadly at Leona. "I can't believe I'm saying this, but yes, I'll do it. I'll audition! Just as soon as I get dressed...."

"That's great!" Leona checked the clock again: 8.56pm. There was barely enough time to get to the auditorium, let alone to change....

She reached for Lily's hands again and held them tight in hers. "You know, it's almost nine o'clock. Why don't you just go how you are? I mean, really, what's more perfect for a singing audition than musical PJs?"

Lily shivered again and nodded. "Sure.... Whatever you say...."

They burst in just as the final auditioner was coming off the stage.

"Thank you, Anya. I have to say, you've brought on your yodelling routine a long way from last year."

"Thanks, Ms Frasier," said the curly-haired girl. "So ... you'll post the results tomorrow?"

"Correct. Outside Kettlekern Hall."

"Yoo-hoo! Ms Frasier!" Leona called as she guided Lily down the aisle. "You have one more auditioner!"

The music teacher turned and lifted her eyebrows in an expression of happy surprise.

"Lily! You're back...." She checked her watch. "And look at that, just in time." She paused to sniff, her chin raised. "Mmm! Warm apple pie! I hope there's some left in the dining hall."

The girl who was holding a flugelhorn stared at Lily as she passed her. "Are you wearing *pyjamas*?" she asked.

Lily glanced down, then back at Leona, who simply waved her towards the stage.

"Just get up there and sing!" Leona told her. "What's wrong with pyjamas?" she barked at the girl.

"Nothing! Nothing at all. I just wondered where she got them, that's all. Do you think maybe they make some with flugelhorns instead of notes?"

"So you're going to sing?" Ms Frasier asked, as Lily climbed on to the stage.

Lily nodded.

"Do you need music?"

Lily shook her head.

"Well, then, please go ahead," said the teacher.

Hesitant, Lily gulped down a breath.

Leona smiled up at her from the aisle. "You can do it!" she mouthed silently. "It's your gift to share!"

Lily nodded at her, took another breath, and started to sing.

CHAPTER
10

"You made it!" Leona dragged Lily to the bulletin board outside Kettlekern Hall.

Lily read the sheet. "I made it...."

"Of course you did!" Leona said. Now all Lily had to do was win for Leona's mission to be complete! "Hey, what's wrong?" She looked at Lily. "Are you okay? Are you going to faint?"

"I don't know if I can do it."

"Do what?" Leona asked.

"Sing."

Leona was confused. "Of course you can *sing*! Your voice is amazing!"

"I mean in front of the whole school. I know what you said about it being a gift and all...." Lily gnawed her lip and sighed. "But just thinking about it now, it feels almost like a curse."

"Oh, no, no! It *is* a gift! Just wait until you're up there onstage, and you'll see!" Leona closed her eyes, envisioning herself in that spot exactly. "When all those eyes are on *you*! And everyone is just holding their breath, waiting to hear what you can do! *Lily?*" Leona opened her eyes to find her Wisher propped up, pale, against the wall.

"Okay, maybe I didn't say that quite right.... Come on." She linked arms with Lily.

"Where are we going?"

"We're going back to our room, and you're going to practise your song, and I'm going to record you and play it back so you can hear how good you are!"

Back in their room, Leona took out her Star-Zap and did exactly that.

"Ooh! Is that a new phone? What kind is it?" Lily asked as soon as she saw it.

"Um ... this? It's newish, yes...." Leona said. "It's a ... prototype.... My dad is in the business," she added. "You'll probably have one yourself next year. Anyway! We didn't come here to compare phones. We came here to rehearse. How about you sing that song you sang at the audition, and you can hear how you sound when you're done. I love to do that! Oh, but first ... let's do some vocal warm-ups. Do you ever do those? No? You should!"

She led Lily in a series of hummed scales and lip rolls, all while they twisted and bent their knees to loosen up.

"It sounds like we're singing underwater!" Lily laughed. The exercises not only warmed up Lily's voice; they warmed up her mood, too.

When they were done, Leona made Lily stand in front of her mirror and handed her a brush. "Too bad you don't have a stage in here, or at least a microphone. Oh, well. That'll come at the talent show, I guess."

Lily sang her song through once, and Leona played it back.

"So...?" Leona said. "How did that sound to you?"

"Pretty good," Lily answered through a proud, spreading smile.

"And how did it *feel*?" Leona asked. She nodded at Lily's hairbrush. "Into the microphone, please!" she joked.

Lily giggled and held her brush to her chin. "It felt pretty good, too."

★

For Leona, the rest of the time was a blur of classes and homework and meals. She knew it was all part of the mission, since a Star Darling's first job was to fit in. But it was all so ... well, so *boring* ... except for the precious time she found to help Lily rehearse. And even then, while it was great to see her Wisher grow more confident, it was hard – incredibly hard – to sit back and watch another singer 'take the starlight', as they say. Leona had a whole new appreciation for teachers, like Professor Dolores Raye, who could easily do things for you but instead sat on their wish energy and let you try and try again.

In their spare time, Lily taught Leona how to play a game called tennis. It was played on a court with lines painted on it and a net going across the centre. Each player stood on opposite sides of the net and used something called a racket to hit a small bouncy yellow ball back and forth. It was very difficult to do, and Leona thought, *How can Wishlings possibly think this is fun?*

The rackets each had a handle and a big oval-shaped top with very tight strings that the ball could bounce off. The goal was to keep hitting the ball – either before it bounced at all or after only one bounce – over the net and within the lines.

"So you've never played tennis before?" Lily asked, even though it was quite obvious.

"Uh, no – I never have," Leona said.

"You look a little confused," Lily said. "Even if you haven't played, I'm sure you've seen it on television."

"Oh, yes, of course. But I just didn't know it was so difficult," Leona said, trying to sound like she was telling the truth. Making a Wishworld wish come true was challenge enough, but keeping her cover was exhausting work! *I will have to teach the Star Darlings how to play this game*, she thought.

On the morning of the talent show, Leona headed with Lily to the dining hall for breakfast, which Leona had decided was the best meal of the day. She'd grown especially fond of a certain cereal full of colourful marshmallows in assorted shapes. She even filled a little plastic bag with some to take back home. Whether she would share it with the other Star Darlings, however, was still up in the stars.

"Oh! French toast again!" Leona remarked, reading the blackboard posted at the front of the hot-food counter. "I liked that! *Mmm!* Let's get some! Remind me, what's that spice they use called again?"

"Cinnamon?"

"Right! Cinnamon. So good! And the syrup is...?"

"Maple?"

"Right! Maple! Yum!"

"Where is it that you come from again?"

"Who? Me? Um ... Sp-sp-something. Let's eat!" She grabbed a tray.

They joined the queue, then, all of a sudden, they heard someone behind them begin to hum a familiar tune.

"Hey, that's your song!" Leona said, nudging Lily.

They both turned to discover Talia, along with her two dance mates. Since the auditions, Leona had tried to spend as little time around those girls as possible, which hadn't been that hard, as it turned out. They shared few classes, and even in those, the girls kept mostly to themselves. She'd noticed them once – no, maybe twice – passing by the music room where Lily rehearsed. The dance studio the group used was in the same building, so it made sense, she supposed.

"You know she's singing that song, right?" said Leona. "In the talent show tonight?"

"Oh, we know. We've heard her singing it," said Talia.

Her friends nodded.

No one smiled.

"Good song, right?" Leona said brightly.

Talia made a sour face, which she shared with Kasey. Adeline still seemed like she didn't agree with them.

"Yeah. Great song." Talia snickered. "If you're, like, in primary school, I guess."

Leona looked at Lily, whose face had turned a painful red.

Leona bristled. "So then why are you humming it?" she asked Talia, who shrugged.

"It's just one of those songs – like all those baby songs – that gets stuck in your head, I guess. I *wish* I could stop." Talia groaned. Then she started to sing it herself – *horribly*, on purpose – and soon the whole breakfast queue was laughing.

"Oh, just ignore her," Leona said, turning back to Lily. "Oh, no, please don't cry!" she said. Lily's chin was quivering dangerously. "I'm really not good around tears!"

Leona was relieved, therefore, to see Lily's older sister striding up from the end of the queue. Leona sighed and stepped back, making room for the older girl to swoop in and comfort Lily.

Lily looked up, too, hopefully. She sniffed and even smiled. Her sister, though, maintained a straight, stern mouth and hard, disappointed eyes.

"Really, Lily? You're going to *cry* now? You're in high school. Act like it." She shook her head and turned away, grumbling, "When are you going to grow up?"

Lily stood there, biting her lip to hold back a fresh reservoir of tears. But it only worked for a starmin. Then the dam broke and they started to spill. Lily was out of the queue and through the door before Leona could say "bless my stars".

Leona cast a longing look at the warm platter of French toast waiting to be served. It might be the last chance she had to get some on Wishworld ... but that was how wish granting worked.

Leona found Lily in the quad sitting huddled on a bench.

"So, as I was saying, don't listen to those girls." Leona slid in next to Lily and gently nudged her, hoping to get her to look up. "They're just jealous and trying to psych you out because they know how good you are."

"Well, it worked, 'cause I'm out," Lily said softly. She kept her head down as she spoke.

"Just wait till tonight, when they watch you win first place. I've got to take a holo-p– I mean picture – of that Talia's face! Wait. *What?*" Leona's head whipped round. "You're quitting? But you can't! It's your wish!" She didn't say, *I can't fail on my first Wish Mission.* But in her head, she was screaming it.

"I can't get up there. You heard my sister. I'm a baby," Lily said.

"She didn't say that...."

"She didn't have to. That's what she meant. Just once, I wish she'd take my side, like you do. But she never will."

"So show her she's wrong!" said Leona. "Show those Fake-a-Moves, too!"

"I want to," said Lily, "but I can't. Not all by myself. I thought I could do it.... I mean, you've helped me so much.... And it's funny, I've never had a problem singing in a group, in the chorus. But it's just too ... too scary to think of singing up onstage, in front of people, all alone."

Leona threw her head back. She didn't know how to reply. How could she change Lily's mind when what she was saying made no sense? Leona had always loved singing – *alone*. She was drawn to the starlight like ... like one of those fluttery Wishworld insects that looked like moonmoths to the big round bulb outside the front door of their Havisham dorm. Of course, she didn't mind backing singers. They made her feel like more of a superstar, in fact. And duets could be fun ... with the right Starling. But choruses? Ugh. They were always saying things like "Try to blend in more", and "Stop stepping out of your row!" Still, Leona had to do something to get Lily's wish back on track. The success of the mission depended on it.

And she'd been so busy she hadn't taken any time to try to figure out what her special talent was. Maybe that was a mistake. Maybe that was just what she needed to make this wish come true.... Then a thought suddenly tickled the corner of Leona's mind. "Are you saying that you would do the talent show if you didn't have to sing all by yourself?"

"What do you mean?"

"I mean ... what if I got up there and sang with you? Would you do the talent show then?"

"Uh ... well ... I don't know...."

"You wouldn't be alone," Leona reminded her.

"No." Lily nodded. "You're right.... Would you?" She smiled shyly. "Would you really do that for me?"

"You bet your stars!" roared Leona. "Um, I mean ... I guess so. If it would help *you* get up there and sing, and show all these girls how talented – and brave – you are, then yes." Leona bowed humbly. "I'd be most honoured to help."

CHAPTER
11

Leona was just about to follow Lily into the arts building to practise their duet when she glimpsed (was it? Yes!) a hot white flash across the sky. It was their free period before lunch and after a class Leona had come to like a lot: History of the Ancient World. Her mind was still reeling, in fact, from that day's lesson about a place called Greece, where they believed in many gods, including one named Helios, who drove a golden chariot across the sky each day. And this, the Greeks believed, was how the sun moved from east to west.

Leona wondered if Lady Stella or any of her teachers were familiar with this Wishling myth. She added it to her Wishworld Observations just in case they weren't. She also wondered where such a myth had come from.

Could maybe – just maybe – some ancient Starling have shared their means of Wishworld travel with some ancient Greek? And maybe, as in a game of holo-phone, a few details were changed? Leona could see how it might have happened. Stories were fickle things. She had to sit on her hands to keep from raising one and saying, "That sun chariot stuff is crazy, but you really can ride a shooting star!"

But back to the flash, which Leona would have missed if a small, furry grey Wishworld creature hadn't scampered across the path in front of her and made her stop and hop back. As soon as the creature reached the grass, it sat up on its hind legs and stared at her, twitching its fluffy tail as if to wave her a Wishling hello.

"Hello, to you, little Wishworld ..." *Hmm* ... Leona tried to remember what the species was called. A 'squid'? A 'squirt'? A squ-something ... And that was when she had noticed the silvery burst.

If it had been that wonderful Wishling holiday when they lit up the sky with colourful, sparkling explosions, Leona would have thought it was one of those. But since it was not a holiday, Leona guessed the source at once.

Lily poked her head out of the door of the arts building. "Are you coming?"

"Yes!" Leona waved. "I mean, I am ... in just a second. I think...." What did she think? "I think I left something ... somewhere.... You go on and start rehearsing, and I'll be there as soon as I can."

Lily shrugged and withdrew into the building while Leona leaped over the friendly, wide-eyed Wishworld creature and dashed around the arts building, to the edge of the school grounds.

"Well, I'll be starstruck!" she said. She was right. She was not alone!

"Vega!" She ran up to give her fellow Star Darling a hug. "What on Wishworld are you doing here?"

"Leona! Star greetings!" Her eyes widened as she took in Leona's sparkly self. "Wow, are you sure no one else but us sees us sparkly?"

Leona shrugged. "That's what Sage and Libby said. Plus, no one's mentioned it!"

Vega grimaced. "And that outfit! Is that *tartan*? Oh, no! Did your Wishworld Outfit Selector break?"

"Oh, this." Leona looked down. She'd almost got used to the whole jacket-tie-kilt thing. "It's a 'uniform'. Everyone wears them at this school, I'm afraid."

"Oh, dear ... Star apologies," said Vega. She took Leona's hands in hers. "At least it's just for a little while. Is that the wish you're here to grant? To get rid of them?"

"No. I wondered that, too, at first." Leona shook her head and shrugged. "But why are *you* here?" she asked Vega. "My mission's almost done!"

Vega's nose scrunched and her mouth twisted. "Yes, about that ..." she began. "Actually, the thing is ... your wish ... it actually appears to be a bit off track.... Not that it's your fault or anything!" she added quickly. "We all know this is one of the hardest jobs in the universe! What can you expect? We're all new to wish granting, after all, and it's happened every time."

"Not this time!" declared Leona. "Sorry to disappoint you, Vega, but my wish couldn't be more sure of being granted. Everything's going startacularly well! I've identified my Wisher and her wish, and in –" she checked her Star-Zap – "approximately nine starhours, her wish will be officially granted. I don't know what kind of signals Lady Stella was receiving, but feel free to take your star home and tell her they were wrong. Or stay! That would be stellar!" She gave Vega's hands a squeeze. "Then you can be here to see me not only rock this wish, but –" she shimmied excitedly – "sing!"

Vega tilted her head. "This wish ... are you sure about it?"

"What do you mean? Of course I'm sure!"

"I mean ... are you sure the wish is truly your *Wisher's* wish?"

"Like I said, of course I'm sure. Who else's would it be?"

"I don't know ..." said Vega. "All I know is that the energy levels were indicating that something was amiss. That's why I'm here. Maybe if I stay, I can help you figure it out."

Gently, Leona let Vega's hands go. "Suit yourself. But you'll have to change." She nodded at Vega's silk-smooth blue shift.

"Right...." Vega looked down at her pretty new dress and made a face. "But how? I don't think I have anything like your uniform in my Wishworld Outfit Selector." She checked. "Not even close."

"I know," said Leona. "We'll just say you're visiting. That you're just thinking of going to this school. But let's hurry!" She cheerfully linked her arm with Vega's. "My Wisher's waiting for me to rehearse!"

Vega followed Leona to the music building. "Nice place, this school," she remarked. "You know, it reminds me a little of Old Prism."

"Really?" Leona glanced around. "They have buildings there like this?" She had never been to Old Prism, one of the oldest settlements on Starland, although it was a popular place for tourists to go. She couldn't imagine any architecture on Starland being so rectangular, though. It simply wasn't the kind of shape Starlings naturally thought of.

"I said 'a little'," Vega clarified. "I meant in the way Old Prism is historic. This place is old for Wishworld, too, isn't it?"

"Is it?" Leona shrugged.

Vega pointed at a plaque to the side of the door.

" 'Winterbottom Hall'," Leona read. " 'Built 1792'. I don't know.... That's only a few hydrong staryears. That's not so very old."

"I know, but on Wishworld that's lifetimes," said Vega. "It's like a star era to us."

Inside, they found Lily already rehearsing in one of the soundproof rooms. Leona and Vega caught half a chorus before Lily noticed them and stopped.

"Oh, please go on!" said Vega, applauding. "That sounded beautiful!"

"It really did!" Leona said. "Now just wait till you hear our duet! Oh, by the way, Lily, this is Vega ... a friend of mine from home."

"Hi," said Lily shyly. "So, are you thinking of going to school here, too?"

"Er ... maybe ..." Vega's slender shoulders rose slightly. "We'll see how it goes. So, you two are singing a duet...?"

"Yes." Lily nodded. "For the talent show tonight."

Leona grinned and laid her arm across Lily's shoulder. "It was my idea!" she proudly explained. "It was the only way I could convince her to do the show. Crazy thing is she'd been wishing to do it but came this close to backing out!"

"Really." Vega raised a thin blue eyebrow. "How ... generous of you."

"Oh, it was nothing!" Leona squeezed Lily's shoulder. "We should probably get started," she said then. She pointed with her other hand to a stool in the corner. "You might want to sit over there."

Vega perched on the seat and listened until a bell rang to signal the end of the period. Lily had a P.E. class to go to then. Technically, Leona did, too. But Vega begged her to give her a tour of the campus, and Leona happily said she would.

"So they take Physical Energy here on Wishworld, too?" asked Vega after Lily had gone off to her class.

"No, no. The 'E' is for 'education', not 'energy'," explained Leona. "It's not the same at all. Even though yesterday we did play a game a bit like star ball. They call it basketball, I think. You *have* to use your hands, though, which I kept forgetting. It was so hard! Not that I was ever that good at star ball, either." She winked. "So, what would you like to see first? Oh, I know! Let me show you the dining hall. It's rather dreary compared to Starling Academy's, but there's all the lemonade you can drink!"

"Is that the drink Professor Elara Ursa told us about?" asked Vega.

"Yes! You have to try it! It's the most delicious drink! It's sour *and* sweet, all at the same time!"

"Kind of like puckerup juice?"

"A little. But without the spice ... and the sparkle, too. Here, I'll show you!" Leona veered to the right and dragged Vega along with her.

Vega hung back, though. "Maybe later. I didn't *really* want a tour. Your Countdown Clock is ticking, and I think we need to talk."

"About what?" Leona frowned.

Vega pointed back to the music building. "About that," she said. "This duet ... are you sure about it?"

"Sure, I'm sure!" Leona said. "Like I said, it's the only way I could get Lily to do the show."

She explained how hard even getting Lily to sing a duet with her had been after the mean things some Wishlings had said. "And it wasn't just these jealous girls – it was her own sister, too. Do you think all Wishling starkin are like this?" Leona asked.

"Moon and stars!" said Vega. "I hope not!"

Leona couldn't help thinking of her own starkin: her two brothers, who were older and already out of school, and her two younger sisters, who were students back in Flairfield, still living at home. Leona had hoped they would follow her to Starling Academy, but neither one had even applied. Just like the rest of her family, they were perfectly content with small-town life. Still, Leona holo-called them often on her Star-Zap, and she loved hearing about life at home. In fact, since she'd been on Wishworld, it was the thing she had missed the most.

She suddenly wondered what her family thought now that stardays had passed since their last holo-call. If only Leona could have told them about her mission ... but Lady Stella's plan was too top secret to be shared with anyone. She hoped when their mission was over, she'd be able to tell them everything. And she hoped, thanks to her, that starday was coming very soon.

"Please, Vega. Trust me. I know what I'm doing here. Now, do you want to try some lemonade or don't you? It's up to you."

CHAPTER
12

At seven o'clock sharp, the curtain went up in the auditorium and Ms Frasier took the stage.

"Welcome to Havisham Academy's 65th annual talent show!" she announced. "I think you're all in for quite a treat! We have talent this year we've never had before!

"First, of course, I'd like to thank our distinguished panel of judges. Judges, will you please stand up?"

A line of adult Wishlings stood up in the first row and turned, waving and grinning. Leona recognized several teachers as well as the headmistress who had welcomed her to the school.

"As you know, the judges will be awarding a first prize," Ms Frasier went on, "but, really, everyone who performs is a winner tonight. I hope, therefore, that you'll show them all the respect they so deserve. Now, without any further ado, ladies, may I please present our first performers, who were last year's winners ... and the year before that, too: Talia, Kasey and Adeline – otherwise known as Make-a-Move."

The students in the audience applauded politely as Talia and her friends ran onstage. Leona did not miss the icy glare Talia shot at Lily. On Starland, it was known as giving someone a solar flare.

"Ignore her," Leona told Lily.

"I'm trying," she said. "I really am." Lily looked down at her glittering gold outfit: lamé leggings and a sequined top, plus shiny gold patent-leather lace-up ankle boots. Next she smiled at Leona's ensemble, a mirror image of her own. "I still don't know where you got these awesome costumes," she said.

"Oh, you know." Leona shrugged. Naturally, she had used her Wishworld Outfit Selector, but she had to keep that to herself. "They are pretty stellar, aren't they! But hey! We're stars! What else would we wear?"

Onstage, Make-a-Move was making moves, each member at a slightly different speed. Their smiles, however, were huge, and their ponytails swung impressively.

"So they've really won the past two years?" said Leona.

Lily nodded. "Mm-hmm."

Just then, Hannah, the girl with the lifelike doll, walked up beside them. She held her partner, Dolly, in her arms. "Wow! You two look like real rock stars!" she told Leona and Lily while Dolly checked them out.

"We try," Leona told her. Lily blushed. At the same time, the music ended and the crowd broke into cheers.

"Oh, I hope they don't win again," muttered Hannah as the dancers bowed and high-fived off the stage.

No one else congratulated them. A few girls rolled their eyes. Dolly whispered something into Hannah's ear that made her eyes grow wide.

"Really, Dolly! I can't believe you would say that! That's so rude!" Hannah laughed.

If Make-a-Move cared, though, they certainly didn't show it.

"Who wants to quit right now?" Talia said.

Fortunately for everyone, Ms Frasier soon appeared and herded the act out of the stage door. "Girls," she announced, "after you've performed, please go out and join the audience so it's not so crowded back here. Next up, Hannah and Dolly!"

"We're ready!" Dolly declared.

Leona surveyed the other performers backstage, all waiting their turns to go on. There were a few other dancers, including one with shiny black shoes that clicked whenever the soles tapped the floor.

Several girls with instruments had made the show, as well. Along with the girl with the flugelhorn, there were a pianist and a tall copper-haired girl who blew into a thin silver tube.

Ms Frasier had been firm about not having non-performers backstage, so Vega sat in the audience along with the rest of the school. Leona could see her from the edge of the wings, but Vega could not see Leona. Vega looked anxious, wringing her hands in her lap. Leona wished she could run down and tell her to stop. Her mission was bound for success! But no, she was going on soon and had to save her voice. She needed to focus on her performance! Wait ... that sounded wrong.

Leona tightly squeezed her eyes closed, trying to unscramble her tangled thoughts.

Aha. She knew what she needed.

"I'll be right back," she told Lily, dashing off to find some privacy.

"Wait! Don't leave me!" Lily said. She followed Leona to a quiet corner backstage.

Leona closed her eyes, took a deep breath, and let everything else melt away. "You are a star. Light up the world," she murmured three times purposefully.

"What did you say?" asked Lily.

Leona turned to Lily. "It's just something I say sometimes that helps me ... you know ... find myself."

"How does it go exactly?" asked Lily.

"Like this: 'You are a star. Light up the world.'" She touched Lily's arm. "Try it. Go on. It really works."

Lily did.

"How do you feel?"

"I feel ... better." Lily's chin rose a little higher. Her shoulders seemed to relax. "I can do this!" she said, smiling at herself.

Leona also felt better, though not quite the way she'd planned.

"Lily! Leona!" Ms Frasier motioned from the edge of the stage. By that time, half a dozen more acts had gone on and come off. "Places, please. Charlotte is almost done, and you two are on next."

"Ready?" said Leona. She linked her arm with Lily's in the Starling way.

"Ready!"

"Then let's get out there and sing! I – I mean we – I mean *you*, most of all, are so winning first place! Get ready for your dream to come true!"

That brought a smile from Lily. "Oh, I don't care if we win. Do you? I'm just happy to be doing this at all.

When we met, I was just wishing to have the courage not to chicken out the way I did last year. I'd love to show my sister that I can do it, you know, and maybe make her a little proud of me for once."

Leona stared at Lily. Now everything made perfect sense. She knew what she had to do.

The shiny-shoed dancer *tap-a-tapped* off, waving her top hat and cane. Ms Frasier returned to the stage with two microphone stands.

"Thank you, Charlotte! Now, please welcome your next performers, Lily and Leona!"

Leona stepped in front of one mic while Lily took the other one. Leona drank in the round of applause like it was a tall, cold glass of lemonade.

She smiled down at Vega and even waved, hoping to get her to smile back. At the same time, she tried to ignore Talia and her friends. Unfortunately, they were working way too hard at making themselves impossible to miss. Rather than clapping, they were giggling and whispering loud enough for everyone to hear. It was all Leona could do not to use her energy and shut them up with a flick of her wrist. They were lucky she kept her hands clenched round the microphone instead.

"Thank you! Thank you, everyone! Really, you're too kind! Hey, how about a round of applause for our

real star of the night, Ms Frasier. After all, without her,
none of us would even be here. Am I right?"

Leona led the crowd in another round of applause,
to the teacher's delight. Then she took a deep breath and
leaned back over the mic to add one more thing.

"Now, I know the programme lists our next act as a
duet ... but the truth is I'm not out here to perform. I'm
just here to introduce my friend Lily, who'll be singing a
solo for you all."

A collective gasp rose from the crowd as Leona
stepped away. The loudest gasp by far, though, came
from Lily, who spun towards Leona in disbelief.

"I can't!" she mouthed.

"Yes, you can," Leona mouthed back. And she had
to, Leona knew. Vega was right. For Lily's true wish
to be granted, she had to prove to herself that she had
the courage to get up there and sing alone. Leona had
got much too carried away with the idea of singing
along with her. But there would be plenty of time for
performing back on Starland. This was the time for Lily,
and Lily alone, to shine in the starlight.

Leona gazed deep into Lily's eyes. "You are a star. Light
up the world," she murmured, pointing to her own heart.

Lily bit down on her lip and slowly nodded. She
stepped closer to the mic. At that moment, something

happened. Lily changed, like the sky when the sun breaks through the clouds. And it took place so quickly that Leona wasn't even ready for the fountain of wish energy that gushed out.

It poured out at her in a blindingly brilliant arc – blindingly brilliant, that is, to Leona and Vega. The roomful of Wishlings had no idea. All they were aware of was Lily standing in the spotlight, getting ready to sing for them.

"So sing already!" someone hollered in a shrill voice.

"We're waiting!" someone else howled.

Leona tore her eyes from the flow of wish energy to scan the audience for the source. She knew, of course, who it was before she found them: Talia and her friends.

Leona turned back to Lily, whose face had frozen. Her wish energy flow had all but stopped. Leona knew she should be worried about her mission's success then, but all she could think about was her Wisher and her Wisher's feelings, and how she could make those bullies stop. She was just about to raise her hands and use energy to dump water on them when someone else jumped up.

"Hey! That's my sister! And she'll sing when she's ready. Show a little respect. You can do it, Lily!" called her sister. "Take all the time you like."

"Yeah!" others yelled, and a chorus of agreement rose around her, followed by a round of supportive applause. Lily's eyes, meanwhile, filled with clear, happy Wishling tears as she and her sister shared a smile.

ZOOWWWWWHOOOSHHHHH!

If Leona had been slow to capture the first surge of wish energy, she nearly missed the next as it burst towards her like a tidal wave in a whole new, even more spectacular rainbow. It was simply startacular.

CHAPTER
13

"**Moon and stars!** That was starmendous, Leona! Truly!" Vega gushed. She punctuated her compliment with a warm, impulsive hug.

"Star salutations," said Leona. "Especially for opening my eyes."

They stood in a corner of the lobby, where everyone had gathered after the show. Everyone, that is, but Make-a-Move, whose members had stormed off as soon as the judges' votes were tallied and Ms Frasier announced the results. Talia and her friends had not won first place, which surprised nobody but them. That award had gone to Lily, whose performance had earned the sole standing ovation of the night. Nor had they won second. That had gone to the pianist. Dolly and Hannah had come away with third. Make-a-Move had earned something else, however; they had been disqualified – "for behaviour unbecoming to students of Havisham Academy, or anywhere else," Ms Frasier had announced.

"Oh, you would have figured out what to do on your own, I bet," Vega told Leona. "But I'm glad that I could help."

"I don't know if I would have." Leona sighed. "I got pretty excited about singing up there. Even when I realized what helping Lily's wish come true really meant, it was hard to step out of the starlight and let her shine, alone. It would have been so startastic to sing with her, up onstage on Wishworld.... It would have been the chance of a lifetime."

"Well, clearly you're meant to be a Star Darling, thinking about others and not yourself. I just hope that when it's my turn, I do half as well. Literally!" said Vega. "You captured two wishes' worth of energy!"

Leona rubbed her Wish Pendant proudly while Vega pulled her Star-Zap out. "So, should we head back?"

Leona held back. "Now?"

Her eyes skimmed past Vega to Lily, who stood at the other end of the room. She looked thrilled but overwhelmed by the throng of classmates surrounding her.

Their eyes met and Lily's hand shot up in a swift 'I need you' wave.

"We *can't* go yet," Leona told Vega. "I haven't even said goodbye."

Goodbye.... The word hung in front of Leona like a dark, unexpected cloud. Somehow, this part of a mission had never occurred to her before. She'd been too busy, she supposed. And now that the time had come, she wasn't ready. Not at all.

"Of course," Vega told her. "Star apologies. You're absolutely right. But you should hurry."

"I will!" said Leona. "Wait here. I won't be long."

Leona reached Lily and threw her arms round her. "Congratulations! You were so great!"

"Thanks! Ooh!" Lily giggled and shuddered. "Wow, there's a lot of static in the air these days."

"Oh, sorry." Leona let her go. "I knew you could do it!" she went on.

"Well, that makes one of us." Lily laughed. "When you said I was singing a solo, I honestly thought I was going to faint!"

"Yes ... but then you did it! You found the power in yourself to make your dreams come true! And I bet you can't wait to do it again! Tell me singing up there onstage wasn't the best feeling you ever had!"

"Actually ..." Lily started, but just then, her big sister appeared.

The older girl smiled at both Lily and Leona. "You're new, aren't you?" she said.

Leona nodded.

"Well, I'm glad you're here. Thanks for being such a good friend to Lily. There aren't a lot of girls at this school who would have helped her the way you did. Honestly, I didn't think I'd ever see her get up onstage."

"Well, it won't be the last time!" said Leona. "Especially when she knows you have her back."

"I know, but I'm not always going to be there. I graduate this year. That's why I keep trying to make Lily stand up for herself. If you don't," she told Lily, "who will?"

"I know." Lily nodded. Then, suddenly, she stood straighter, as if an idea had sparked in her mind. "In fact, I'm going to stand up for myself right now.... You owe me a duet!" she declared, turning to Leona. "We can't let all that rehearsing go to waste. Hey, what if we formed a band!"

"A band? That's the best idea ev–" Leona started to say when a tug on her elbow made her stop. She looked down to see Vega staring up at her with wide 'are you out of your mind?' eyes.

"What I mean is, *you* should form a band," Leona clarified. "You'd be a great lead singer! And every school needs at least one band! But ... I don't think I can start it with you. In fact, it's impossible."

"Why?"

"Uh ... because ... well, because ... I didn't want to seem like a show-off, so I didn't tell you this before ... but I actually just signed a recording deal, and I have to go cut an album ... tonight."

"Really?" Lily's jaw fell open, and her sister's did the same.

Leona nodded matter-of-factly. "Would I lie about something like that?"

"Tonight?"

"I'm afraid so. At least, that's what my agent tells me." She smiled at Vega. "Right ... agent? Isn't that really why you came?"

"Uh ... sure," Vega said slowly.

"You're her *agent*?" Lily asked.

Vega shrugged. "I know ... it's crazy, isn't it?"

"I think it's awesome!" said Lily. "Wow.... Now it's really too bad we didn't sing together," she joked. "I almost sang with a real star."

Lily's sister spoke up. "I'd love to hear you. In fact, I bet everyone would."

Leona felt herself blush, Wishling style, as Vega hooked her arm.

"Too bad we have a *flight* to catch," Vega said meaningfully.

"Wait." Leona held her ground. "Okay. I'll do it." She slipped her arm from Vega's and took hold of Lily's hands. "Let's go and sing that duet. You talked me into it. But let's do it out under the stars!" she said. "Have you ever sung there before? Oh, you'll love it! It's the best!"

CHAPTER
14

Leona had realized her Wishworld goodbye would be hard, but it was even worse than she had feared. She probably would never get to see Lily again. Not in person, at least. There was always the chance, Leona supposed, of catching a glimpse of her from the Wishworld Observatory. But with seven billion Wishlings on Wishworld, the odds were atom-slim. Still, Leona swore to herself she would try and try and try until she did. Lily was sure to do something great with her talent on Wishworld, and Leona was *not* going to miss it.

She tried to keep this in mind as she said farewell to Lily after their duet.

"Text me!" Lily told her.

"I'll try ..." Leona said. But, of course, as soon as she hugged her goodbye, Lily's memory and those of all the rest of the students at Havisham Academy were erased.

"Just remember what a great mission this was," Vega said to comfort her as they got ready for their trip home.

"Think how much you just accomplished towards helping Starland," Vega went on. "You're not just a Star Darling, you know. You're a true star-hero."

"Star salutations," Leona said gratefully. "I couldn't have done it without you, you know."

Vega smiled. "Okay. See you back home!"

"Why, Leona! Vega! What in the universe happened to you two?" Lady Stella said, ushering the newly arrived Star Darlings into her office and helping each into a chair.

Both were pale, for Starlings, and their glows flickered on and off. The stars in Leona's hair had burned out and needed to be charged.

"I don't know," Leona panted. "Something went wrong on the trip back. All of a sudden, my star started to stall. Then it started to drift. It was terrible! Luckily, Vega was there to pick me up ... otherwise –" she caught her breath – "I don't know what I would have done...."

"Well, I was there." Vega patted Leona's hand. "We just need a starmin to recover our glows."

Leona bolted up straight, suddenly energized. Her trip had been stressful, but now she was home. She placed her hand over her Wish Pendant proudly. She could only imagine how much positive energy her single Wish Pendant now contained!

Vega sat up, too. "You should have seen her, Lady Stella! She thought she was just going to grant one wish and she ended up granting two!"

"Two wishes!" gasped Lady Stella. Her face lit up in thrilled surprise. "Two wishes. Heavenly stars. This was a most exceptional mission, it seems. Come. Let us summon the other Star Darlings to the Wish-House and collect your most well-earned and deserved Wish Blossom. That is, if you're up to it. Or perhaps you need a bit more time...."

"Oh, no!" Leona sprang out of her chair. "Let's do this! I'm ready!"

The alert went out and the Star Darlings rushed from wherever they were to the headmistress's office. Leona glowed in delight at all their attention and in anticipation of the honour to come.

Leona was happiest to see Ophelia, and Ophelia clearly felt the same.

"So how did it go?" Ophelia asked her.

"Startastic! I'll tell you all about it later! How about you?"

Ophelia shrugged. "We can talk about that later, as well.... This moment is for you."

Lady Stella walked over, gently cradling the Wish Orb. She solemnly placed it in Leona's eager hands. It glowed in her grasp and her pulse quickened in anticipation. Everyone held their breath, waiting for the stunning moment of transformation. But there was nothing.

A panicky feeling started to rise in Leona's chest. It was unfamiliar and decidedly unpleasant. "What's going on?" she asked, looking at Lady Stella for reassurance.

But Lady Stella looked puzzled and confused. "I don't understand," she said, inspecting the Wish Orb. "It should have happened by now."

But it had not.

"Ew!" exclaimed Gemma. "What's wrong with your Wish Pendant, Leona? Everyone look! It's all burned up!"

"*Gemma!*" Tessa whispered harshly, scowling at her sister. Still, what Gemma had said was true.

The thing on Leona's wrist barely resembled her Wish Pendant, although it was basically the same size and shape. Instead of gleaming gold, however, it was gnarled and as black as soot.

"Leona! What did you do?" murmured Astra.

"I don't know!" Leona wailed. "Really! It was perfectly fine when we got back to Starland. You know that. You saw it, too. I don't know how or when this could have happened! I don't know what I could have done!"

"Did something go wrong on your mission?" asked Adora. She was trying to be helpful, but the question still stung.

"No!" said Leona. "It went starmendously! Unless ... oh, no ..." she moaned. "Unless I overloaded it ... unless the energy from two wishes was too much for my Wish Pendant to absorb."

"Moon and stars! Are you saying you granted two wishes on your mission?" said Cassie. "Can you even do that, Lady Stella?"

The headmistress, who by now stood over Leona, stared at her Wish Pendant in wide-eyed alarm. "Indeed, you can. It's entirely possible, though exceedingly rare. When it has happened, though, the positive wish energy collected has been more than double what a typical wish brings in." Carefully, she lifted the arm bearing Leona's Wish Pendant and examined it closely, turning it slowly right and left. "What's happened here simply makes no sense. The magic of Wish Pendants comes from their limitless capacity for positive energy. Exceeding it is impossible, as astrophysics has well proved. No, I do not believe that's what happened here. Granting two wishes would never cause this kind of Wish Pendant destruction."

"Then what did?" Leona wailed. She pulled her wrist back and shook her cuff in mortification and disgust. "Oh, wormholes! I can't believe all that wonderful energy I collected is now wasted! You all should have seen it!" she went on. "I should have come right back, as soon as I had it. I should never have stayed to sing that song...."

"You stayed to sing a *song*?" said Astra.

Leona hung her head and nodded. "With my Wisher."

Astra and a few others traded 'there you have it' eyes.

Sage spoke up. "I stayed for a little while, too, after I collected my wish energy. And it wasn't a problem at all. You don't know what it's like," she told Astra and the other Star Darlings. "You haven't been to Wishworld yet. Goodbyes are the hardest part."

"Yes, I don't believe that affected your Wish Pendant, either, Leona," said Lady Stella. "You mustn't blame yourself. I would be shocked if there was anything a Star Darling could do to render her Wish Pendant useless like this. There's no such thing as too much positive wish energy, nor would any well-meaning action cause such harm. Perhaps," she went on, "there was a flaw in your Wish Pendant that no one noticed, or a defect that could not be detected until it was used. I assure you, this is no fault of yours, but merely a malfunction that will prove most helpful, in due course."

"But how?" growled Leona. "How can a filthy, burned-up Wish Pendant help anyone?"

The headmistress smiled kindly, almost as if she had a plan. "If I may ..." Leona's skin tingled as Lady Stella grasped the cuff and slid it from her wrist. "It's very simple," she explained. "I'm going to have Professor Dolores Raye examine this and determine precisely what went wrong. There's no one in the universe more knowledgeable about wish energy, after all. And, as we know, knowledge is power. Her findings will help us design corrections to prevent this from happening again. Fear not, Leona. Despite this tragedy, your mission was not in vain."

"Shall I take it to her?"

Lady Stella turned, as did the Star Darlings, to see Lady Cordial emerging from the shadows of the Wish-Cavern.

"Why, star salutations, Lady Cordial," said the headmistress. She bowed and held the cuff out for her colleague to receive.

"My s-s-s-stars!" Lady Cordial winced as she regarded it. She clucked in dismay. "How dreadful...."

"I know," Lady Stella agreed.

"Though I suppose disasters such as this are to be expected in such a new and risky endeavour ... with such young, inexperienced St-St-Starlings...."

Lady Cordial's eyes stayed focused on the Wish Pendant, but her words hit Leona like a spear. Leona felt Vega's arm wrap round her, but she shrugged it off and stepped away. Lady Stella had made her feel better for a starmin, but Lady Cordial was right. She'd been given the chance of a lifetime and ruined everything. She didn't deserve her friend's comfort or Lady Stella's or anyone's. Maybe she didn't even deserve to be a Star Darling any more. Just like Scarlet.

The evening was still young, and everything on Starland was just beginning to reach its maximum glow, but Leona had no interest in any of the hundreds of nightly activities the students at Starling Academy normally enjoyed. The last thing she wanted to do was stargaze or play neon energy ball or collect globerbeems in crystal jars. She didn't even feel like singing. All she wanted to do was go back to her room in the Big Dipper Dorm and be alone for as long as she could. She knew Ophelia would be there eventually. Maybe by that time she'd want to talk.

She held her hand up to the scanner in the middle of her door.

"Welcome, Leona," the Bot-Bot voice greeted her as the panel glowed a bright blue. Smoothly, the door slid open, and Leona slipped into her room.

She debated for a starsec whether to leave the lights low. Finally, with a heavy sigh, she blinked to turn them up and chase the shadows from the room.

"Scarlet!"

"Star apologies," said Scarlet, stepping out from the corner where the dark had hidden her. "I didn't mean to startle you."

"You didn't startle me. You scared my stars off! What are you doing here? How did you get in?"

"I used the hand scanner. It still works." Scarlet held up her hand. "And I really thought we needed to talk." She glanced quickly around the room. "No one else is coming, right? Are we all alone? Something really weird is going on, Leona –"

"Go!" Leona raised her arm and jabbed her finger at the door. "I don't want to talk now, Scarlet. I don't want to do *anything*. Can't you tell I'm not in the mood?" She clenched her jaw and crossed her arms. The empty spot where her Wish Pendant had been looked pale and dull. "I've had the worst starday ever, and talking to you is not going to help. If anyone should know how I'm feeling now, it should be you, I think."

"But –"

"Please!" Leona growled. "We can talk about the band or whatever you want tomorrow. Stay in it or not. But this isn't your room any more, so you have no right to be in here. Technically, you're trespassing. Do you want me to send a holo-signal to security? Because I will."

Scarlet blew her fringe in frustration but didn't argue any more. Instead, she tugged the collar of her star-studded jacket and stomped towards the door. As it slid open, she glanced over her shoulder. There was a dark spark in her eyes that was new. "Fine. I'll go," she said. "But just know you're making a mistake."

"Well, it won't be the first one," Leona retorted, whooshing the door closed behind Scarlet. She threw herself down on her bed. She had somehow ruined what should have been her finest moment. What was she going to do?

Glossary

Bad Wish Orbs: Orbs that are a result of bad or selfish wishes made on Wishworld. These grow dark and warped and are quickly sent to the Negative Energy Facility.

Big Dipper Dormitory: Where third- and fourth-year students live in Starling Academy.

Blushbelle: A pink flower with a sweetly spicy scent. Libby's favourite flower.

Bot-Bot: A Starland robot. There are Bot-Bot guards, chefs, waiters, deliverers and guides on Starland.

Bright Day: The date a Starling is born, celebrated each year like Wishling birthdays.

Celestial Café: Starling Academy's outstanding cafeteria.

Cosmic Transporter: The moving pavement system that transports students across the Starling Academy campus.

Countdown Clock: A timing device on a Starling's Star-Zap; it lets them know how much time is left on a Wish Mission, which coincides with when the Wish Orb will fade.

Crystal Mountains: The most beautiful mountains on Starland. They are located across the lake from Starling Academy.

Cyber Journal: Where the Star Darlings record their Wishworld observations.

Druderwomp: An edible barrel-like bush capable of pulling its roots up and rolling like a tumbleweed, then planting itself again.

Flairfield: Leona's hometown. This pleasant, sleepy little town has a population of 30,000 and a charming downtown area.

Flash Vertical Mover: A mode of transportation similar to a Wishling lift, only superfast.

Flutterfocus: A Starland creature similar to a Wishworld butterfly but with illuminated wings.

Galactical: Having a negative overreaction.

Gamma chip clusters: A crunchy, sweet and salty snack.

Garble greens: A Starland vegetable similar to spinach.

Glimmerworm: The larval stage of the glimmerbug. It spins a beautiful sparkly cocoon from its silk. Empty cocoons are used to create fine textiles.

Glion: A gentle Starland creature similar in appearance to a Wishworld lion, but with a multicoloured glowing mane.

Globerbeem: A Starland creature similar to a Wishworld firefly, only more sparkly.

Good Wish Orbs: Orbs that are the result of positive wishes made on Wishworld. They are planted in Wish-Houses.

Halo Hall: The building where Starling Academy classes are held.

Holo-letter: A letter from one Starling to another that is a hologram. There are also holo-billboards, holo-books, holo-cards, holo-communications, holo-diaries, holo-flyers, holo-papers, holo-pictures and holo-placecards – anything that would be made of paper on Wishworld is a hologram on Starland.

Holo-phone: A Starland game – much like the Wishworld game Chinese Whispers – in which a phrase is passed from one Starling to another and the last Starling says it out loud. The final message is often markedly different from the initial one, much to everyone's amusement.

Hydrong: The equivalent of a Wishworld hundred.

Impossible Wish Orbs: Orbs that are the result of wishes made on Wishworld that are beyond the power of Starlings to grant.

Lightfall: The time of day when the sun begins to set and everything on Starland glows its brightest.

Lightning Lounge: The place where students relax and socialize.

Little Dipper Dormitory: Where first- and second-year students live.

Mirror Mantra: A saying specific to each Star Darling that, when recited, gives her (and her Wisher) reassurance and strength. When a Starling recites her Mirror Mantra while looking in a mirror, she will see her true appearance reflected.

Moonfeather: A material commonly used for stuffing pillows, coats and toys. It is harvested from the moonfeather bush.

Moonium: The equivalent of a Wishworld million.

Moonmoth: Large glowing creatures, which are attracted to light like Wishworld moths.

Moon shot: A very slight possibility.

Mustardia: A plant whose bright yellow blossoms are often puréed and used in savoury sauces.

Old Prism: One of Starland's original settlements. Filled with beautiful buildings that once housed Starland's founding mothers, it's a place with a lot of town pride and a rich history. It has become a folksy tourist destination by day, but at night it's a sleepy little town. Cassie's hometown.

Ozziefruit: Sweet plum-sized indigo fruit that grows on pink-leaved trees. It is usually eaten raw or cooked into pies. Starling Academy has an ozziefruit orchard.

Ranker: A small machine that judges competitions and picks the winners. Its fair program eliminates favouritism.

Safety starglasses: Worn by Starlings to protect their eyes when in close proximity to a shooting star.

Shooting stars: Speeding stars that Starlings can latch on to and ride to Wishworld.

Solar flare: A mean look designed to intimidate.

Solar metal: A common, inexpensive kind of metal.

StarBook: A cyber hang out where Starlings post pictures and opinions.

Star Caves: The caverns underneath Starling Academy where the Star Darlings' secret Wish-Cavern is located.

Starf: A Starling expression of dismay.

Starjade: A smooth, green semi-precious stone.

Starkin: The Starling word for siblings.

Starland: The irregularly-shaped world where Starlings live. It is veiled by a bright yellow glow that, from a distance, makes it look like a star.

Starland City: The largest city on Starland, also its capital. Sage, Libby and Adora's hometown.

Starlicious: Tasty, delicious.

Starlight: When all eyes are on a Starling, they are said to be 'in the starlight'.

Starling Academy: The most prestigious all-girl four-year boarding school for wish granting on Starland.

Starlings: Glowing beings with sparkly skin who live on Starland.

Star marble: An extra-luminescent natural stone used for walls and floors.

Starmin: Sixty starsecs (or seconds) on Starland; the equivalent of a Wishworld minute.

Star Quad: The central part of the Starling Academy campus.

Star salutations: A Starling expression of thanks.

Stars crossed: An expression meaning 'hoping for a favourable outcome'. Similar to the Wishworld expression 'fingers crossed'.

Starsec: A brief period of time, similar to a Wishworld second.

Starweed: A plant with thin, emerald-green leaves, often eaten cooked in soups or raw in salads.

Star Wranglers: Starlings whose job is to lasso a shooting star to transport Starlings to Wishworld.

Star-Zap: The ultimate smartphone that Starlings use for all communications. It has myriad features.

Sunspots: A Starling expression of dismay.

Toothlight: A high-tech gadget that Starlings use to clean their teeth.

Wish Blossom: The bloom that appears from a Wish Orb after its wish is granted.

Wish energy: The positive energy that is released when a wish is granted. Wish energy powers everything on Starland.

Wish energy manipulation: The ability to mentally harness wish energy to perform physical acts, like turning off lights, closing doors, etc.

Wisher: The Wishling who has made the wish that is being granted.

Wish-House: The place where Wish Orbs are planted and cared for until they sparkle.

Wishlings: The inhabitants of Wishworld.

Wish Mission: The task Starlings undertake when they travel to Wishworld to help grant a wish.

Wish Orb: The form a wish takes on Wishworld before travelling to Starland. It will grow and sparkle when it's time to grant the wish.

Wish Pendant: A gadget that absorbs and transports wish energy, helps Starlings locate their Wishers, and changes a Starling's appearance. Each Wish Pendant holds a different special power for its Star Darling.

Wish-Watcher: A Starling whose job is to observe the Good Wish Orbs until they glow, indicating that they are ready to be granted.

Wishworld: The planet that Starland relies on for wish energy. The beings on Wishworld know it by another name – Earth.

Wishworld Outfit Selector: A program on each Star-Zap that accesses Wishworld fashions for Starlings to wear to blend in.

Wormholes: A Starling expression of dismay.

Zing: A traditional Starling breakfast drink. It can be enjoyed hot or iced.

Zoomberry: Small, sweetly tart berries that grow in abundance on Starland.

Acknowledgements

It is impossible to list all of our gratitude, but we will try.

Our most precious gift and greatest teacher, Halo; we love you more than there are stars in the sky ... punashaku. To the rest of our crazy, awesome, unique tribe, thank you for teaching us to go for our dreams. Integrity. Strength. Love. Foundation. Family. Grateful. Mimi Muldoon – from your star doodling to naming our Star Darlings, your artistry, unconditional love and inspiration is infinite. Didi Muldoon – your belief and support in us is only matched by your fierce protection and massive-hearted guidance. Gail. Queen G. Your business sense and witchy wisdom are legendary. Frank – you are missed and we know you are watching over us all. Along with Tutu, Nana and Deda, who are always present, gently guiding us in spirit. To our colourful, totally genius, and bananas siblings – Patrick, Moon, Diva and Dweezil – there is more creativity and humour in those four names than most people experience in a lifetime. Blessed. To our magical nieces – Mathilda, Zola, Ceylon and Mia – the Star Darlings adore you and so do we. Our witchy cuzzie fairy godmothers – Ane and Gina. Our fairy fashion godfather, Paris. Teeta and Freddy – we love you so much. And our four-legged fur babies – Sandwich, Luna, Figgy and Pinky Star.

The incredible Barry Waldo. Our SD partner. Sent to us from above in perfect timing. Your expertise and friendship are beyond words. We love you and Gary to the moon and back. Long live the manifestation room!

Catherine Daly – the stars shined brightly upon us the day we aligned with you. Your talent and inspiration are otherworldly; our appreciation cannot be expressed in words. Many heartfelt hugs for you and the adorable Oonagh.

To our beloved Disney family. Thank you for believing in us. Wendy Lefkon, our master guide and friend through this entire journey. Stephanie Lurie, for being the first to believe in Star Darlings. Suzanne Murphy, who helped every step of the way. Jeanne Mosure, we fell in love with you the first time we met and Star Darlings wouldn't be what it is without you. Andrew Sugerman, thank you so much for all your support.

Our team ... Devon (pony pants) and our Monsterfoot crew – so grateful. Richard Scheltinga – our angel and protector. Chris Abramson – thank you! Special appreciation to Richard Thompson, John LaViolette, Swanna, Mario and Sam.

To our friends old and new – we are so grateful to be on this rad journey that is life with you all. Fay. Jorja. Chandra. Sananda. Sandy. Kathryn. Louise. What wisdom and strength you share. Ruth, Mike, and the rest of our magical Wagon Wheel bunch – how lucky we are. How inspiring you are. We love you.

Last – we have immeasurable gratitude for every person we've met along our journey, for all the good and the bad; it is all a gift. From the bottom of our hearts we thank you for touching our lives.

Shana Muldoon Zappa is a jewellery designer and writer who was born and raised in Los Angeles. With an endless imagination, a passion to inspire positivity through her many artistic endeavours, and her background in fashion, Shana created Star Darlings. She and her husband, Ahmet Zappa, collaborated on Star Darlings especially for their magical little girl and biggest inspiration, Halo Violetta Zappa.

Ahmet Zappa is the *New York Times* best-selling author of *Because I'm Your Dad* and *The Monstrous Memoirs of a Mighty McFearless*. He writes and produces films and television shows and loves pancakes, unicorns and making funny faces for Halo and Shana.

Vega and the Fashion Disaster

Vega sat on her neatly made bed, staring at the holo-crossword puzzle projected into the air above her Star-Zap. With two flicks of her wrist, she switched the position of two answers, then frowned and returned them to their original places. She nodded, finally satisfied. It was perfect. Vega loved creating puzzles almost as much as she enjoyed solving them. She appreciated crosswords, riddles, puzzles, brainteasers, mazes and games – anything that challenged her and made her think in a fun and interesting way.

With another flick of the wrist, she erased all the answers, leaving the clues and a blank grid, ready to be filled in. She took a look at her handiwork and sighed. The real joy in creating a puzzle was sharing it with someone. She wished she could send it to her best friend from home, Enna, who loved games just as much as she did. The two girls had even made up a secret holo-alphabet they had both memorized so they could communicate privately. What looked like gibberish to their classmates back at Kaleidoscope Falls Elementary might be a complex message about after-school plans or the guest list for Enna's upcoming Bright Day party.

Sure, Vega belonged to Starling Academy's Puzzle Club, which met after school every Dododay and was filled with like-minded students. It was the first club she had joined since arriving at the school two years earlier. But the secret nature of the Star Darlings made this crossword something she could not share with anyone except them. So there were only 11 girls she could share it with, and, unfortunately, none of them were particularly interested in brainteasers. In fact, they seemed to think Vega's obsession was a little weird. Just a starweek or two earlier, she and Leona had found themselves sitting across from each other at lunchtime in the Celestial Café. After they had ordered their meals from the hovering Bot-Bot waiter, Vega had turned to Leona excitedly and said, "Let's guess whose food will arrive first!" and Leona had just laughed. "Everything is a game to you, Vega, isn't it?" she said. Vega had blinked at her in surprise. It was – and why not? Games made life more interesting. She didn't get why the other girls didn't understand that. Not that she wasn't serious-minded – quite the contrary: she was as focused on her studies as a Starling could be. But she could make studying into a game, too.

As she recalled the conversation, Vega realized that was one of the last times she had heard Leona laugh. Her Wish Mission had been a terrible disappointment. Although she had successfully granted her Wisher's wish, Leona's Wish Pendant had malfunctioned, and when she had returned to Starland, she had discovered it was blackened and burned-looking. As a result, Leona hadn't collected a single drop of wish energy. The usually vivacious girl had been sad and withdrawn ever since. Lady Stella had done her best to convince her it wasn't her fault, but Leona was set on blaming herself.

Lady Stella told everyone to keep attending class (including their special Star Darlings-only class at the end of each school day), learning their lessons, and going on their Wish Missions as planned. The headmistress would be working with some leading wish energy scientists and some trusted faculty members to figure out what had gone wrong with Leona's Wish Pendant and how to fix it. Hopefully they would figure it out soon.